4th & Girl

D1733082

max monroe

4th & Girl
A Mavericks Tackle Love Novel
Published by Max Monroe LLC © 2018, Max Monroe

ISBN-13: 9781984368959

Editing by Silently Correcting Your Grammar
Formatting by Champagne Book Design
Cover Design by Peter Alderweireld
Photo Credit: Wander Aguiar

Dedication

To Wes Lancaster and the New York Mavericks: Not gonna lie, sometimes, you guys were a pain in the ass. The whole lot of you are cocky and demanding, and you almost never do what we tell you.
But despite all of that, we love you guys.
Thank you for making 2018 such a fun year.

To Sia: We might have retired the wigs, but you and those black-and-blond mops will always hold a special place in our hearts.

To Kim Holden and Gemma Hitchen: We kind of sort of stole your names, mashed them together, and put them in this book. But, if anything, that should show you how much we adore you.
You're our favorite real-life angels.

intro

Leo

In my opinion, in football, there isn't a more badass position than shutdown cornerback.

What makes *my* position so badass? Well, I have to be agile and quick and have a natural instinct for the game. My footwork has to be on point, and my speed has to be unmatched. I have to cover, read, adjust, and break on the ball. This position, *my position,* is one of the biggest anchors of pass defense plays.

What does all of that football lingo mean?

It means I'm vital.

It means I'm the guy who will stop a quarterback's touchdown pass.

I'm the man who won't let the best wide receivers in the league get their greedy hands on the ball.

Last year, my college record was nearly unheard of. I held opposing QBs to a 47.9 rating when they tried to throw the ball to the man I was covering.

Basically, I was *the* badass in one of the toughest positions in the league.

And now, as one of the newest first-round draft picks for the New York Mavericks, I'm the guy with everything to prove.

I can either be the big hero, or I can be the guy who loses the fucking game.

My reputation is on the line, my nearly flawless career in college taunting me in the background to live up to it, and if there's one thing I need to do, it's focus.

But life's got other plans.

I should have my mind on my money—and my money on my mind—but the only thing I can seem to think of these days is the mystery girl I met at one of the team's very first group activities.

Blond hair.

Long lashes.

Criminally blue eyes.

She's petite and awkward, and she's completely fucking up the plan.

But it's too late to second-guess.

And it's sure as fuck too late to go back.

Once my mind is fixated on something, there's no stopping me.

I have my eye on the bombshell prize, and I won't settle for anything less than victory.

Good thing I'm at my best when the pressure's on.

Chapter One

Gemma

My dad would shit himself if he knew I was hanging out with the Mavericks today, I thought to myself as I took in the large logo painted across a wall inside the New York Mavericks' stadium's brand-spanking-new medical facility and lab.

Except, *gah*. He probably wouldn't.

Yes, Lon Holden—*otherwise known as my dear old dad*—was one of the Mavericks' biggest fanboys, but he probably wouldn't have been too thrilled to find out his daughter's job of the day included collecting urine from his favorite football players.

Not only was that *not* every father's big dream for his little girl, but *my* father's dream for *me* was pretty much the opposite of this.

Truthfully, it was the opposite of everything I did these days.

He wanted me to follow in his footsteps and his father's footsteps and his grandfather's footsteps and become an engineer just like the rest of the Holden clan.

The big plan? To eventually take over our family's engineering consulting firm.

I'd been on board. I'd been dutiful. I'd been everything he wanted me to be until about a year ago.

And then I'd dropped out of college one year away from getting my degree and shot it all up in flames.

One month into my senior year, while I sat inside Advanced Engineering and Professor Serbin prattled on and on about thermodynamics and the ways they were vital to my future profession, I had an epiphany.

An "I can't fucking do this anymore" kind of lightbulb moment.

It wasn't out of rebellion, laziness, or modern Hollywood-style dreams of becoming "Insta-famous." I just couldn't continue to strive for a degree that bored me senseless, and I couldn't pretend to be someone I wasn't.

Twenty-four hours later and I'd officially dropped all of my classes and taken a leave of absence from NYU's engineering program.

The aftermath wasn't pretty.

My dad had a meltdown.

My mom calmly tried to talk me out of it, and then, when that didn't work, had a crying jag in the bathroom with a glass of whiskey and the cigarettes she thought no one knew she hid in there.

And Grandpa Joe had questioned whether or not I'd fallen ill with a mental breakdown.

Fallen ill with a mental breakdown, his words exactly.

Like a mental breakdown was the equivalent of catching the flu.

Not likely, Grandpa Joe.

But I couldn't be mad at my grandfather's reaction or his words. It had been the exact kind of response you'd expect to get from a man who had been raised in the "pick yourself up by your bootstraps and get the fuck over it" generation.

I, on the other hand, was a millennial. The generation Grandpa Joe's generation pretty much despised and predicted would be the end of civilization as we knew it.

I called bullshit to his dramatic take on an entire generation, but even if Judgment Day was near, I refused to spend the rest of my time between now and then dying the slow death of pursuing a career I hated.

Of course, now, here I was. Twenty-three with no future prospects for a longstanding career to speak of. Completely uncertain of what I wanted to do or who I wanted to be. Instead of climbing the corporate ladder or padding my 401K, I was working for Star Temps—a temp agency that sent me to all kinds of odds and ends jobs—and paying the necessary bills.

Dog walking. Housecleaning. Secretarial work. You name it, and I'd done it.

And the current task of the day? Collecting professional football players' urine for drug testing.

Apparently, this was an annual formality at the start of every Mavericks season.

I watched quietly as Lisa, my coworker of the day, stacked up fresh urine cups on the laboratory counter. With careful fingers, she piled them into some sort of neurotic tower.

Honestly, they appeared just fine to me in the cardboard box they'd been delivered in, but I kept my questions to myself.

With her perfect yet severe brown bun on the top of her head and her pristine white scrubs, Lisa appeared to be a woman on a medical mission, and far be it for me to put a damper on her pee-cup parade.

"How long have you been a medical assistant?" she asked, and I swallowed against the nerves doing a gyrating dance on their way up from my belly.

Technically, I wasn't really supposed to be doing this temp job. But, Mable, the old lady who ran Star Temps, was short on medical assistants and figured what the Mavericks didn't know wouldn't hurt them.

Completely illegal, I was sure, but I wasn't exactly in the financial position to be declining a paycheck. And, if I was being honest, the Mavericks compensated greatly for being in charge of their football players' piss.

Lisa glanced at me over her shoulder, and I cleared my throat.

"Um…not long," I finally answered, strategically sugarcoating the fact that I had zero medical background. Hell, the only time I'd ever stepped foot inside a hospital was back in high school when I'd thought being a candy striper would look good on my college resume.

It'd only taken two hours into my shift to realize medical shit was not for me.

Watching an old guy puke up green Jell-O I had to clean up, and then promptly ask for another serving, hadn't been my idea of a fun extracurricular activity.

Not that I didn't like helping people, I just preferred to do it with a little less bodily fluid involved.

Funny, given today's activities, how that'd worked out for me.

"Do you have a full-time job somewhere?" Lisa questioned as she continued to stack. One cup, two cups, she paid careful attention to detail, going so far as to make sure all of the seams lined up perfectly. My messy personality nearly had a seizure watching it.

Playing Twenty Questions when you almost positively didn't know any of the answers was a little like high-stakes gambling with no experience, but not answering wasn't a normal human behavior and pretty much went against all social skills. My only option was to play nice with my coworker and hope to Jesus it didn't end up getting me fired.

"No, not really," I answered semi-honestly. "I'm more of a fly by the seat of my pants kind of gal."

"Oh," she said and glanced at me over her shoulder again. "What doctor's office did you do your medical assisting clinicals at?"

Medical assisting clinicals? Were those a thing? Was this a test? There should have been some sort of warning if there were going to be trick questions! Fucking hell, Detective Lisa was hot on my heels. I could only assume she wasn't making up crap like I was.

"Uh…Doctor…Shepherd's."

I didn't personally know a Dr. Shepherd, but I knew Derek Shepherd from *Grey's Anatomy* real flipping well. I mean, eleven years' worth of Thursdays pretty much made me a Derek Shepherd expert, if you asked me.

May he rest in peace.

"Dr. Shepherd?" she asked. "I don't know a Dr. Shepherd. What kind of practice does he run?"

The key to a lie was to stick as close to the truth as possible. Or so I'd been told. So, that's what I did. I stuck to the truth. Or, in this case, the plot of a TV show.

"He's a neurosurgeon."

"A neurosurgeon?" Lisa's eyes perked up like a stoner who'd just been told weed was legal. "Wow. That's so interesting."

Not that I know anything about being a stoner or smoking weed.
Well, besides that one year in college, but doesn't everyone experiment their freshman year?
Just me? Okay, yeah, forget I said anything...

"Yep," I agreed. And seriously, it *was* interesting. Who hadn't loved watching Dr. Shepherd perform brain surgery? Before his shocking death—*which I'm still pissed about*—he'd been the best damn neurosurgeon Seattle Grace, hell, even the country, had ever seen.

"Wow," she said again. "Did you get to see any surgeries?"

"Oh yeah." I waved a nonchalant hand in the air. "All the time."

If her eyes had gotten any brighter, I could've turned the lights out and saved the Mavericks on electricity.

In my humble and maybe a tad bit judgmental opinion, this chick needed to get out a little more. I mean, dollar beer nights at Frankie's in Brooklyn would've really given her medical-assistant-focused-mind a run for its money.

You didn't even need to drink the cheap beer to have a good time.

The last time I was there, I watched two guys fistfight over which *Jersey Shore* character was hotter—*I'm a JWoww fan myself*—and a girl who could've been Courtney Love's doppelgänger flashed her boobs so some guy with a goatee would play Miley Cyrus's *Party in the USA* on the jukebox.

"Did you get to do a lot of blood draws?" Lisa asked, and I silently wondered if this was what the next two weeks of working with her would be like. Of course, her eyes did that thing again where they lit up like someone just handed her a winning lotto ticket.

I started to fear if I gave her any more excitement, she'd channel Meg Ryan in *When Harry Met Sally*—only this time, it wouldn't be fake.

I'll have what she's having? No thank you, Lisa.

But to deny her more medical pleasure felt like a sin, so I just rolled with it.

"Oh yeah," I answered. "Blood, brains, you name it, and I collected it."

Her eyes popped big and wide. *"You collected brains?"*

Whoops. In the name of Lisa's medical O, I'd officially taken it too far.

"I'm kidding," I backpedaled, and the look of relief in her eyes was evident. "Just a little neuro humor."

"You scared me for a minute there," she said with a hand to her chest. "I thought maybe this Dr. Shepherd was running an unethical practice."

Derek Shepherd unethical? That's blasphemy! The man had lived his life for his career!

I felt outraged for all of Seattle Grace and Shonda Rhimes.

"Dr. Shepherd was the very best man I've ever known," I said, and my voice turned soft. "Well, until he died, that is. May he rest in peace."

Lisa's eyes turned gentle. "He died?"

"Yeah," I said, and I swear to God, the trauma of Season 11, Episode 21 hit me straight in all the feels. "Terrible accident," I whispered and had to blink back the tears. "No one, and I mean, *no one*, saw it coming."

Damn you, Shonda Rhimes!

"That's horrible," Lisa said, and I nodded, just solemn little tilt forward of my head.

"Tell me about it. Thursday nights haven't been the same since."

"Thursday nights?" Lisa, the goddamn supersleuth, asked, and I kind of felt like smacking her.

But I didn't.

Instead, I backpedaled…*again.*

"Uh…we used to, uh…fish on his land every Thursday."

"Wow. Sounds like you two were close."

I nodded again. "You have no idea, Lisa. No idea."

Obviously, I really needed to derail this crazy-train conversation before Ms. Medical Assistant caught onto my lying game.

"So, uh, Lisa," I redirected. "Mind giving me the rundown on how you usually handle these drug tests?"

Quick as a flash, there were her happy, I-love-my-job eyes again, and it didn't take long for my medicine-loving coworker to dive head-first into a conversation that revolved around her favorite things—medical assisting, urine collection, and the potential for blood draws.

By the end of her instructional ramble, I knew two things.

Lisa was one hundred percent type A.

And two, she loved the prospect of medically allowed violence.

Her enthusiasm terrified me a little, and that was why it didn't take long for me to make the executive decision to be the girl who told the players what to do and to collect their urine, and to leave the rest of the technical stuff to Lisa. She could test, she could log, she could do all the shit I wasn't qualified to do anyway. I'd stick to hand-ing out and collecting cups.

The hallway noise got noticeably louder as I crammed infor-mation from the instruction manual on how to collect a proper piss sample as quickly as I could, and my nerves kicked into overdrive.

Sure, Lisa had just instructed me on all this shit, but hells bells, that didn't mean I retained it. If anything, I was more focused on the way her tight bun didn't budge an inch whenever her head moved.

"Looks like we have our first customer of the day," Lisa said less than a minute later, and I looked up to find the most gorgeous set of

baby-blue eyes I'd ever seen in my life. With the rest of the team yucking it up and making more noise than I knew was humanly possible
in the hallway, the first player had apparently found his way inside.

And I thought I had nice blue eyes? Sweet baby Jesus in a man-
ger, this guy's eyes were locked and loaded and prepared to take down
any female in their vicinity.

No shit, I had to blink three times just to make sure they were
real.

Once I realized what I was seeing was, in fact, reality and not
some fantasy born out of medical assisting boredom, I couldn't stop
myself from taking further inventory of the very fine specimen of a
football player standing in the doorway of the lab.

Thick, dark hair.

A faint little scar resting just below his right eye.

Strong, chiseled jaw.

Broad shoulders.

Trim waist.

Toned thighs.

And what I could only assume was the kind of tight ass that
would've had Grandma Louise doing a double take. She might've
died ten years ago, but I felt like this guy's heady gaze held the power
to summon her from the dead.

*Which, yes, I can see where that last bit of commentary may have
been a bit disconcerting. But if you knew Grandma Louise, you'd
understand. The woman's bucket list included Thunder from Down
Under and meeting Dwayne "The Rock" Johnson.
May she rest in peace.*

"Hi, I'm Leo," the guy introduced, and holy hell, even his voice
was stupid sexy. "Leo Landry."

"Hi, Leo," Lisa greeted, apparently too focused on, you know, doing her job to realize we'd just been graced with the sexiest player on
the Mavericks' squad. "Give us just a minute, and we'll get you in and

out of here quickly."

I, on the other hand, was otherwise mute and busy wiping drool from my chin.

Lisa looked at me. I looked at Lisa.

And we repeated that circuit a good three times before a scowl started to form across her thin lips.

Shit. This is my part of the job...

"Oh!" I muttered. "Right." I hopped up from my seat and grabbed a cup from Lisa's Leaning Tower of Pee-sa. "You're obviously here for a reason, and that reason is to pee in one of these here cups so we can collect it," I joked as I made the cup do a little dance across the counter.

Leo tilted his head to the side and watched the cup tip-tap across the surface before bringing his curious eyes back to mine.

A dancing urine cup? Really, Gem? Could you be any more awkward right now?

"For drug testing, obviously," I added. "Not for, like, selling your urine on eBay or something weird like that."

I didn't even bother looking over at Lisa after those words left my lips. It didn't take a genius to anticipate a bulging forehead vein from Ms. Medical Assistant when things like illegal urine auctions were mentioned.

Leo's crystal-blue eyes went a little wide at my words, and it was pretty damn obvious I, Gemma Holden, could be more awkward.

Hell, if I had five more minutes, I'd probably win some kind of Guinness World Record for the mind-blowing ability to shove my entire foot into my mouth. Make it ten minutes and I might've been able to fit both feet.

"So, uh, let's get that urine!" I exclaimed, which, ironically, sounded exactly like a psychopath who was, in fact, attempting to collect a football player's urine to sell it on eBay.

Just shut up and take him to the bathroom before you can make this any more uncomfortable...

"Just follow me," I said and cleared the nerves from my throat.

"And I'll get you out of here lickety-split."

Lickety-split? Jesus Christ. Just stop talking.

With my lips firmly closed, I gestured for Leo to follow me into the small hallway off the lab and led him toward the bathrooms.

He followed with only slight hesitation, and once I spotted the bathroom door, I quickly remembered I hadn't really finished reading the whole "How to Collect a Urine Sample" manual.

Shit. If I screwed this up, Lisa would call the National Board of Medical Assistants and find out I was a fraud.

Could you go to jail for medical assistant fraud?

It wasn't exactly my fault I'd ended up at a job I wasn't qualified for, but Lord knows, Mable would've had my ass if I'd inadvertently let word get out she'd done the sending. She seemed like the kind of woman you found at the temp agency during the week and burning herself with a lighter at a motorcycle rally party on the weekend.

Okay, just focus and keep it short and sweet, I mentally coached myself. *Less is definitely more in this situation.*

"So, uh, here's the place that you pee," I instructed...*like a moron.*

"It looks familiar," Leo said, and a small smirk crested one corner of his mouth. "Pretty sure I've been inside one of these a time or two."

God, even his smirk is sexy...

Stop gawking, Gemma, and give the incredibly handsome man the damn instructions.

"Uh...so...you just pee in this," I said and awkwardly shoved the cup toward his chest. "And when you're done, you're supposed to bring it back out to me without the lid on it so I can ensure it's a *proper urine specimen*," I repeated the words from the manual.

He nodded. "Got it."

Just as he started to step inside the bathroom and shut the door, I remembered one last thing.

"Oh! Shit! And don't flush the toilet either!" I exclaimed as I clumsily stopped the door's momentum with my foot.

And the Medical Assistant of the Day award goes to...not me.

We stared at each other through the small crack in the door, and

I wasn't sure if I wanted to smack my head against said door, or run away and hide behind Lisa's Leaning Tower of Pee-sa.

But, eventually, there was that sexy little smirk again.

If it were up to me, the damn thing should've been illegal.

I mean, who in the hell could work under these kinds of conditions? With this kind of hot, red-blooded male with the prettiest blue eyes I'd ever seen staring back at them?

Certainly not me.

"Pee in cup. Don't flush the toilet. Don't put the lid on the cup, and hand it to you when I'm done," he said, and amusement cradled his voice. "Anything else?" he asked, and I swear on Grandma Louise's grave, those eyes of his turned even bluer with his words.

Fuck if I knew. But it was as far as I'd gotten in the instructional manual.

"That should do it." *I hope.*

I removed my right foot from the door and my left foot from my mouth, and while Leo went into the bathroom and did the damn thing, I slipped on latex gloves and waited outside while I mentally chastised myself.

When he comes back out here, do not make it awkward, Gemma.

Don't say anything like "nice urine" or "good job, buddy" or offer a fucking fist bump.

For the love of God, just collect the urine and do not make it awkward.

Chapter Two

Leo

Piss. Shake. Flush.

It was the normal routine whenever I, or anyone with a dick for that matter, went to the bathroom. So, honestly, I thought I'd have it down.

But this wasn't an ordinary trip for several reasons, and the most glaring excuse of all was the cute blond waiting for me on the other side of the door.

Suddenly, I was self-conscious.

Could she hear me peeing? Was she wondering what was taking me so long? Was this all normal practice for her?

I had no idea, but it was safe to say, thinking about all of it had me rattled.

Plus, I wasn't allowed to flush when I was done, a practice ingrained in me from the time I was a toddler by my type A mother, and the change in routine had me repeating the simple instruction in my head like some kind of bathroom psychopath.

Don't flush, don't flush, don't flush.

Not to mention, the importance of this sample was significant, as the results would determine if I was eligible to play professional football or not.

I wasn't worried—I wasn't into drugs and had barely even imbibed alcohol since high school—but the pressure of everything falling on one tiny cup of piss still niggled.

Thirdly, I didn't think I'd ever had to hand a cup filled with piss to such a pretty woman before.

My nurses during NCAA testing always seemed to be more Helga than Heidi, so mixing thoughts of urine and arousal had never been an issue.

Until *now.*

I guess there's a first time for everything.

Setting the cup carefully on the sink, I washed my hands and dried them with a paper towel before grabbing the specimen and opening the door.

The cute blond's head jerked up from the spot on the tile she'd apparently been focusing on, and I felt a smirk curl the very corner of my mouth.

Maybe I'm not the only one feeling self-conscious.

And good God, she was pretty.

Pint-sized. Big blue eyes. And the kind of full lips most women would pay large amounts of money to recreate with the help of a surgeon.

Not to mention, even with her in a pair of navy blue scrubs, I could tell she had curves.

The exact kind of curves that would make my mouth water and fit perfectly into my big hands.

I felt like a bit of a bastard for even taking that much inventory on the woman who'd been hired by the Mavericks to help process our urine samples, but I couldn't fucking help it. She was perfect in all the ways that drew me in, and with her quirky yet adorable awkwardness, she was imperfect in all the ways that I found endearing.

"All done?" she asked, and my little smirk turned into a smile.

"Yep. I figured it was best to finish up completely rather than come out halfway through."

She blushed at my teasing and looked back to the ground, reaching out for the cup as she did. "Of course. Right."

I shook my head slightly, taking the final two steps necessary to close the distance, and pushed the cylinder into the palm of her hand before releasing.

She exhaled then, looking up from the tile to meet my eyes once more—the connection was powerful.

A stop to time and thought and a powerful lesson in the influence of one simple look.

I was mesmerized.

And then mayhem exploded all at once.

Not as prepared for the exchange as we'd both assumed she was, the cup slipped in her grip and panic suffused her eyes.

As a football player, I was familiar with the slow-motion replay after the action—the one that perfectly pointed out your flawed split-second decision-making—and if there were an ESPN for drug testing, this little ditty would have had prime placement on the highlight reel.

Desperate to stop the cup's descent, she clenched the fingers of her hand quickly, but the force of her reaction only made it worse. Grazing off the cup like a bat on a ball, it sent the specimen flying. The damn thing arced through the air back toward me and shot the pee, *my* pee, out in a monotoned rainbow of fucking disgust.

I jumped back from the tidal wave, but she carried on, lunging for the cup like her life and pride depended on it.

Once, twice, her hand made contact, but after a bobble, a wobble, and an unwelcome hand-bath, the writing was on the wall.

And my piss was on the floor.

Fuck.

"Oh my God," she said, the pitch of her voice rapidly approaching a level only dogs could hear.

My heart bounced in my chest as my brain tried to catch up with the fact that she'd literally just spilled my pee all over herself, but it was a losing battle. The carnage of reality was too unexpected.

"Christ," I muttered involuntarily. Her already manic eyes went wider, and I finally found it in me to sound a little less harsh. *God, she must be mortified.* "Are you okay?"

"Oh? Me? This?" she blathered, circling a gloved hand above the puddle on the floor in between us and the now urine-soaked legs of her scrub pants. "Totally cool. I'll just…uh…"

I looked around as she did, following her around the room like a ping-pong ball, and finally interjected when she didn't finish the thought.

"You want me to try to find you a mop or something?"

"A mop? What do I need a—?" She paused before devolving into a nervous, high-pitched giggle. "Oh yeah. To clean up. Your *pee* that I just dropped." Her head fell back, and her eyes turned skyward. "Kill me now."

I laughed at that, stepping around the puddle between us and awkwardly rubbing a comforting hand down her thankfully dry back.

"Hey, I'm sure it happens all the time."

"Oh *yeah*. This is a regular after school special."

Glancing up briefly to meet my eyes as I put a little more pressure on my comforting stroke, she clenched hers tightly shut and huffed out a breath of air. "I'm guessing you can't go back in and give me another sample?"

"Uh," I said through a laugh. "Not right this second. Tank's empty."

"Greaaaat."

Even in the trauma, she was adorable. A pit in my stomach turned as I searched my mind for a way to make her feel better.

"Listen, can I—"

"Why don't you just take off, okay?" she interrupted me quickly. "I've got to clean up, and…" She sighed. "I know this is important, but I'm sure they'll let you retake it later today or another day or something."

My eyebrows drew together. Despite the importance of the testing and results, I hadn't even thought about when I'd have to make this up.

The only thing I'd thought about since the moment I entered the room was…well, her.

"Look, I can probably—"

"No, no," she interrupted again. "Just go, Leo. I'll handle it." Her voice lowered to a breathy whisper—commentary clearly not meant for me—as she went on. "Lisa is going to *flip* her *shit.*"

With one last lingering look, I did the only thing I could for her. The one thing I desperately *didn't* want to do.

I left.

Without helping. Without getting a name. Without a usable urine sample.

Without a goddamn clue how I found myself thinking continuously about a woman I'd just met.

Chapter Three

Gemma

So, I took an accidental golden shower in some ridiculously hot guy's urine once.

Big deal, right?

I mean, surely, I'd learned my lesson after that horrible scenario. He'd been the first guy in the room, and with time and experience, I'd had plenty of opportunity to gain my footing, and thankfully, a pair of fresh scrubs. I definitely hadn't spilled pee on myself again, that was for damn sure.

"From what they told me, it sounded like you weren't getting the hang of anything besides driving that medical assistant crazy," Mable said, growing a little tired of my shit. She'd called about five minutes ago, an hour before I was due to wake up to head back to the medical assistant gig for day two. And she hadn't held back when she'd broken the news that I'd been relieved of duty.

I'd been pleading my case ever since.

If I was honest, it was a thin case. Like one of those flimsy, plastic phone cases you bought off Amazon on a whim because it was uber cheap and has kittens on it, and then, twenty-four hours into using the damn thing, you realized it's utter junk and did jack shit to protect your device.

Trust me, I did *not* have an Otterbox, will-survive-anything, kind of case to plead in this conversation.

Even *after* I'd spilled a hot guy's pee on myself, I hadn't been too hip to the medical assisting game on my first day on the job. I'd mislabeled shit, knocked down Lisa's tower of pee cups more than once, and three players had to be retested because I'd forgotten to tell them not to flush the toilet.

But it was a two-week temp job that paid forty bucks an hour.

I needed that fucking job. I had a gorgeous Gibson acoustic guitar in my sights, and I was only a few hundred dollars and a couple weeks of eating ramen noodles away from buying it.

"Please, Mable," I begged. "I really need that job."

"Honey, if I sent you back there this morning, they'd have my ass with a stick that is far too big in diameter even for me," she responded in her raspy voice with wayyy too much information.

Good God, I think my ears are bleeding.

Mable was notorious for smoking Marlboro Reds in and out of her office, and the woman's voice was so damn throaty and deep, it sounded like a cat had attempted to remove her vocal cords with its claws. *Especially* when she meant fucking business.

Unwilling to subject myself to any more of her visuals, I finally gave up the fight for the job I sucked at and started exploring other avenues.

"Well, what else do you have available this week?"

"I'll have to get back to you on that. Just stay patient, Gemma. I'm sure I'll find you something in a day or two."

Not the news I want to hear. We ended the call shortly after that, and I tossed my phone back down on my nightstand, shoved my face into my pillow, and groaned.

Not only did I officially have no stream of income, I had nothing to occupy my day. That might seem like a godsend to a lot of people, but ever since I'd dropped out of college, if I wasn't moving, I felt like I was sinking.

It was probably the weight on my shoulders courtesy of disappointed parents and no concrete life plan, but whatever. Busy feet kept me out of the quicksand.

Instead of sulking in bed, I dragged my ass up and headed for the kitchen to make some coffee. As I passed through the living room, I was on a one-woman diatribe about the ridiculousness of getting fired from a job that entailed collecting urine.

"You'd think it'd be simple, Gem. It's only something you've done since you were a toddler. But no. You have to mess up peeing. Who gets fired for collecting urine? Of *all* the things. And you had to do it while God's gift to women—"

"What are you freaking out about?" Abby asked from the couch, and I just about climbed to the damn ceiling in surprise.

"Jesus Christ!" I put a hand to my chest and tried to stop my heart from jumping out of my throat. "You scared the crap out of me!"

"Sorry," she said, but her voice said otherwise.

"When did you get here?"

"Last night."

"You've been here since last night?" I asked and looked around my apartment in confusion. "How did I not know you were here last night?"

She shrugged and sat up on the couch. "You were already asleep when I got here."

"I never should have given you a key," I muttered and headed into the kitchen.

Abby was my best friend and the most unpredictable person I'd ever met in my life.

Honestly, I don't even really know how we met, but ever since that fateful day three or so years ago, she'd become a staple in my life. *And* my apartment.

Her life's activities included working at a coffee shop up the street whenever she felt like it, late nights that revolved around house parties and pub nights, and almost never sleeping at her own place.

She showed up arbitrarily and without permission and made it seem like the most natural thing in the world.

If I stopped and paid homage to her unexpected arrival every time it happened, I'd probably take up an entire year's worth of my life.

Hell, she might as well have been my damn roommate with how often she ended up staying at my place.

She followed me into the kitchen a few moments later, my favorite afghan from Grandma Louise wrapped around her body like a cocoon.

"So, you got fired from collecting urine?" she asked, and I groaned.

"Yeah," I said, pouring fresh water into the coffeemaker before setting it to brew. "I got fired because I inadvertently gave myself a golden shower with some football player's pee."

Abby grinned. "No shit?"

"No shit."

"Damn, girl, you really know how to make a first impression."

"Tell me about it," I muttered and grabbed two cups from the cabinet. "Probably one of the most embarrassing moments of my life."

"What was his name?"

"Whose name?"

"The guy who peed on you."

"Oh my God. He didn't pee on me," I corrected through an incredulous laugh. "His pee just managed to spill out of his cup and onto me."

"Sounds kinky."

"Shut *up*."

"Have you showered since then?"

"Oh my God, Abby!" I exclaimed on a disturbed laugh. "*Of course* I showered since then."

She just grinned, completely unfazed, and continued her original line of questioning. "But seriously, what was his name?"

I sighed. "Leo."

Gorgeous Leo. You'd have to be blind to forget a face or name like that.

Not to mention, you tended to remember the name of the guy whose urine you got to know on an up close and far too personal basis.

"Last name?"

"Landry."

"Leo Landry." She tested his name on her lips. "Sounds like a hot guy's name."

"Well, he wasn't ugly," I admitted. Because, yeah, he wasn't ugly.

Far from it, actually.

"Did you get his number?"

An unexpected and incredulous laugh left my lips. "Um, no. I know it's a shock, but that didn't come up while I was taking an impromptu bath in his urine."

"I should probably be far more grossed out by that than I am," she said, and her voice turned way too wistful and dreamy for a conversation revolving around pee. "You know," she added, "it's a bit romantic in a weird sort of way."

"You're nuts."

"I'm nuts?" she asked, stepping forward to pour herself some coffee without preamble. "I'm not the one running around pouring pee on myself."

"And you're annoying. Remind me again, why do you have a key to my place?"

"Because you love me."

She was right, though I was having a really hard time remembering the whys or hows of my affection at the moment. Abby just grinned at me over her shoulder and headed back into my living room, plopped her ass down onto my couch, and turned on the TV.

"What are your plans for today?" I asked as I poured creamer into my coffee and stirred it in with a spoon. Maybe, if nothing else, I could use her as a distraction.

"Probably go into work for a bit. Not sure yet, though." She shrugged. "What about you?"

"Well, I was supposed to go to work, but that's obviously not an option."

"You know what we should do?"

"What?"

"Go see that new Bradley Cooper movie."

I scrunched up my nose. "But I thought you had to work?"

"Meh. I'll go in tomorrow." She shrugged again and took a sip from her mug.

"How do you still have a job there?" I asked and sat down beside her.

"Because my espresso brings all the boys to the yard."

I rolled my eyes. "You're literally the most random person I know."

"You're preaching to the choir, girlfriend," she said with a grin. "Only one year away from finishing an engineering degree and making six figures a year, and you said fuck it."

"Yeah, well, that was solely out of self-preservation," I explained.

Which was one hundred percent the truth. It was either I dropped out of college or prepared for an early death born out of boredom less than five years into the job.

Call me crazy, but I wanted to live past thirty, thank you very much.

A little grin crested the corners of Abby's mouth as she looked at me over her cup of coffee. "*And* because you're supposed to be a musician, not some stuffy old engineer in an office."

"Let's not get too ahead of ourselves here," I said, rolling my eyes. "I've only played open mic nights. That doesn't make me some kind of music superstar."

Sure, I loved music, but just because you loved something didn't make it a surefire career. The music business was really hard. Demanding and exclusive and nearly impossible to break in to. I couldn't imagine what my parents would think if I told them *music* was the big reason I'd thrown away everything they'd ever dreamed of.

I was pretty sure their heads would explode.

For now, I was more than happy to keep my passion for singing and song-writing a really enjoyable hobby.

"Yeah, but you're crazy good, Gem," Abby insisted, changing the channel to Blue Planet and shifting her body like she was swimming with the damn whales.

"I'm okay," I said honestly, thinking she was distracted enough by nature's bounty to ignore me.

Apparently, she was better than me at multitasking. "Your self-deprecation is starting to annoy me," she remarked with narrowed eyes.

"Yeah, well, you wouldn't have to subject yourself to it if you didn't magically show up in my apartment like David fucking Blaine."

In true Abby fashion, she ignored me completely.

"So, a matinee date with Bradley Cooper?" she asked. I heaved a sigh and then, finally, shrugged.

"Why the hell not."

It wasn't like I had anything else to do.

Unemployed, unoccupied, and underfunded. If I had any hopes of laying hands on that Gibson guitar anytime soon, I'd have to be willing to take whatever Mable sent my way.

Good thing I was so damn determined.

Too bad you can't say the same for your hands when it comes to keeping a hot dude's pee off your clothes…

Ugh. Apparently, my inner self-conscious had gone full-on snarky bitch overnight.

But, thankfully, I was resilient and fully prepared to handle the mental blows. My pride might've been temporarily shot to shit, but that didn't mean I would let it consume me.

Bradley Cooper, on the other hand? One ticket and a large popcorn, please.

Chapter Four

Leo

Never in my life had I been so excited to give another urine sample, and never would I be again, I was certain.

It wasn't like an all-expenses-paid trip to Hawaii or a free Lamborghini, but I had my reasons—*cute, adorably awkward, and so fucking pretty.*

Yeah, I definitely had my reasons.

In fact, last night, I'd spent a hell of a lot of brain power thinking about the blue-eyed blond who'd blundered—or fumbled, if you wanted to get all cutesy and football about it—during our handoff, and Lord Almighty, I was looking forward to seeing her again.

Scratch that, I was *more* than looking forward to it.

I'd mentally kicked myself more than once for leaving when she'd asked me to yesterday, but today, well, it was a glorious chance at redeeming myself.

Hell, I'd even channeled my inner comedian and pondered what jokes I could use to ease any discomfort she might still harbor over the whole embarrassing scene.

If you're looking for pee jokes, urine luck. Ba-dum chuuuu!

Like I said, I'd *pondered* the jokes, but that didn't mean I'd turned into Jerry Seinfeld overnight.

And this morning? Well, I'd spent the majority of it visualizing several much better options for our second exchange than a urine cup fumble.

Assured counter placement. Sink utilization. An undisclosed specimen drop-off location that I could map out for her with scavenger hunt-style clues. Just about anything that avoided another replay of yesterday's piss-falls would do.

I didn't necessarily understand the whys or the hows, but my number one priority revolved around making her feel better.

Anything to put her at ease. *Anything* to find out more about her. Her name. Her number. *Her next available date night.*

Considering our disastrous first introduction, I might have been putting the cart before the horse, but attraction and intrigue were tricky, irrational fuckers, and as much as I liked to control the situation, I wasn't exactly in control of this fixation ride.

Riding shotgun? Of course.

But actually in full control? Not exactly.

The fact remained, I hadn't stopped thinking about the pint-sized bombshell since I'd left the lab after inadvertently marking her scrub pants like a dog on a fire hydrant.

I mean, I was all about swapping some bodily fluids under the right circumstances, but let me tell you, coating a woman in my piss wasn't quite what I had in mind. But maybe, *just maybe*, if I played my cards right, the opportunity for the *right* way would soon follow.

The hall was quiet as I approached the medical wing of the stadium, the complete opposite of yesterday's boisterous laughter the team had obnoxiously bestowed after we'd headed for testing following a meeting with our owner.

This was a seasonal expectation and a task for our jobs, and Wes Lancaster was pretty clear that he expected it to be treated as such. I wouldn't say any of the guys took it seriously to the degree that he'd intended—*I mean, it was just a piss test, for fuck's sake*—but they'd done a better job than me.

Of course, my mishap had been unintentional, but I still didn't like being the guy who'd fucked up. Luckily, I had high hopes for today's venture.

Today, it was just me, one of the only ones who hadn't been able to provide a viable sample on the first go, but second chances are all the rage in movies, so I didn't see why I couldn't put a positive spin on my own.

I'd have a little more time to talk to the medical assistant with the dimpled cheeks, and if nothing else, I'd had a whole extra day to ensure I was properly hydrated.

The overhead fluorescent lights of the lab buzzed as I stepped inside, and I moved my gaze around the room. The space was seemingly empty, but a rotating desk chair belied that possibility with a slow, silent spin.

Either someone had just vacated that chair, or Mavericks Stadium was haunted.

And since I refused to even contemplate the second option, I waited patiently for my cute little blond medical assistant to appear.

Awkwardly unsure of what to do with my hands—*don't worry, I'm never in doubt when there's actually a willing woman around*—I hooked my thumbs into the pockets of my jeans and bounced on my toes.

I was counting the third row of the painted block wall ahead of me when footsteps sounded from around the corner.

Conscious of my appearance, I pulled my hands out of my pockets and crossed my arms at my chest, the picture of cool and casual.

A little smirk set to the corner of my lips, and I was ready for her.

Or so I thought.

Blond hair and dimples rounded the corner, sure, but instead of a Heidi, this time, it was a Hank.

Surprised, I didn't check my verbal filter and blurted, "You're a dude."

He laughed, the muscles of his bicep flexing as he did, and flashed a brilliant set of white teeth at me. "As are you."

I rolled my eyes at myself, knowing how dumb I must have sounded, and tried again. "No, yeah." I chuckled. "Obviously. I just thought it'd be the same person who was here yesterday, and she was not, in fact, a dude."

"Ah," the human Ken doll breathed knowingly. What he assumed was knowingly anyway. Apparently, he had it all worked out in his head, and the arrogance bothered me.

"It's not what you think," I explained like an idiot. "It was just…well, she—*the girl who was here yesterday morning*—well, she dropped my piss and yeah…it was a whole thing," I finished lamely while stumbling over myself as I tried to explain what I realized was an insanely weird set of circumstances.

I mean, not only had my pee spilled all over the pretty little blond, but my interest had followed suit.

And now, here I was, bumbling like a moron while Barbie's real-life boyfriend looked on with amusement.

He laughed, unconvinced by my explanation and completely numb to any kind of compassion. "Spilled the sample, huh? And you're actually surprised she's not here?"

Instantly, I was on edge and one hundred percent offended for her. Not to mention, this prick didn't know anything about her. I narrowed my eyes and stared at the shit-talker. "It's not like she did it on purpose."

"I'm sure she didn't," he said, and sarcasm dripped from his voice.

What a smug fucking bastard.

Sure, I thought the girl was cute, but beyond my obvious bias and fascination, it was pretty damn apparent her bedside manner was miles above this asshole's. I didn't know where Ken got off thinking he was the superior being, but I was officially annoyed by him.

"Specimen collection is pretty much your one and only job in this setting," he added, the fucking know-it-all. "If she can't do that, I'm not surprised she got replaced."

"You know she got replaced?" I asked, and my voice rose a little. Not only was the prick getting on my nerves, he'd touched a sensitive spot in the feel-bad center of my stomach. Being the reason she got fired didn't sit well with me, and getting the news from someone who didn't feel bad for her only twisted the knife deeper.

"Honestly, I have no idea." He shrugged, and if his shoulders could talk, they would've said, *I don't give a shit.* "This is my first day on this job. All I'm saying is, we can assume—"

"We can't assume anything, Ken," I interjected on a snap. "Assuming makes an ass out of you and me both, friend."

His forehead pinched. "My name isn't Ken."

"Might as well be," I said petulantly before turning for the door.

"Hey," he called as I passed over the threshold. "What about your replacement sample?"

I scoffed. *Not on my watch, asshole.* The day I'd give my piss to this annoying as fuck guy would be a cold day in hell.

Apparently, I've lost my mind.

"I'll wait," I said, like I had a goddamn choice. Like this wasn't the edict of my boss and a requirement of the team. Like *I didn't like the guy* was a valid excuse for begging off one of the responsibilities of my job.

Unfortunately, nothing but my righteous indignation and my cute blond's pretty little face registered in that moment.

With one last declaration, I dug my feet in and stood up for every unfairly fired medical assistant in the world.

"I'll wait until the end of time if I have to," I said, and just before I strode out the door, I stole one last glance at Barbie's boyfriend. He looked confused, and fuck, I felt fantastic.

It was glorious.

Well, until about an hour or so later when shit took a turn.

Wes Lancaster got word of my rebellion, and for the first official time in my career, I ended up in my boss's office.

While he read me the riot act and let me know in a very shouty voice that I'd sure as shit be retesting the instant I left his office, I realized pretty quickly that, in the name of a pretty little blond, I'd royally screwed the pooch.

Fucking hell, I'm an idiot.

Way to go, Leo.

Chapter Five

Gemma

Some people ragged on Brooklyn, but I loved it.

It was a melting pot of eccentric characters, families, newlywed couples, single folks like myself, and everything else you could imagine. The commute was easy, and pretty much everything was in walking distance. Bakeries, bars, restaurants, grocery stores—if I needed it, it was there.

Plus, my rent money went a hell of a lot further than it did in Manhattan.

And early fall Sunday mornings in Brooklyn were a bit of a dream.

The air was just brisk enough to get away with a sweater, but not too cold that you needed a scarf or jacket.

The sidewalks were already bustling, but I liked the liveliness of all the calm morning activity.

Ten minutes into my walk back from the grocery store and my phone started ringing inside my purse.

I stopped on the sidewalk, set the bags in my hands on the ground, and fumbled around through my purse.

It took me a minute to find my damn phone because, well, my

purse was like a minefield with bombs of random candy wrappers, old receipts, and emergency tampons, but eventually, I had it within my grasp and pulled it out to find **Incoming Call: Star Temps** flashing on the screen.

Mable.

I silently offered up a prayer to the heavens that she'd found me a new gig.

It had been several weeks since the urine debacle, and I'd been through a bevy of exciting jobs since then.

Customer service for an online company, filer for a law office, a warehouse associate—which was just a fancy name for someone who packs boxes—and most recently, a maintenance specialist in a public restroom. That's right, glory be thy temporary career, I was the woman who kept the countertops dry, the toilets clean, and the paper towels flowing in the Nordstrom's bathroom for a week or so.

Awful restroom jobs be damned, I'd stuck true to my word about taking everything she offered, and as a result, my pretty new guitar baby had pride of place in my apartment. But also, I was once again feeling the pinch of low cash flow.

It was highly unlikely I'd say no to anything she had to offer at that point, or anytime in the near, career-uncertain future for that matter. I just hoped the next assignment would come with more money and a little more insight into what I should really be doing with my life.

"Hey, Mable."

"I've got a job for you, doll," she said by way of greeting. "Pays well."

I fist-pumped the air and silently offered up a prayer to the heavens that "pays well" didn't include tasks that involve collecting bodily fluids or public places where said bodily fluids were disposed of.

"Pays well?" I asked. "How well, exactly?"

"Not as well as the Mavericks thing you screwed up, but that shouldn't be a shock."

She never hesitated to throw that one in my face, no matter the time that had passed.

I sighed and resigned myself to my fate. "What is it?"

"Well…" She took a deep inhale, and I could just picture a cigarette hanging out of her mouth. "It's a seasonal assistant job helping with packing and shipping at a small storefront not too far from your place."

"What kind of store is it?"

"I think they sell stationery…or maybe it's craft supplies? Hell if I know, but they need someone there by tomorrow morning at eight a.m. And they're offering thirty hours a week."

Stationery or craft supplies? It sounded boring as shit. But it was probably better than mopping up bathroom floors and spritzing air freshener to cover the scent of public restroom poop.

"How much does it pay?"

"Thirty bucks an hour, doll."

Okay. Okay. I could definitely deal with packing fucking ribbons and glue guns for thirty bucks an hour.

"How long do they need me?"

"Looks like they want someone to hang around through December."

This could be a steady paycheck for the next three-plus months. I'd have to be brain dead to say no to this thing. And for as much as my parents maybe thought I was a little lacking in brain function thanks to the longevity of my side step from their idea of a picture-perfect future and career, I wasn't mentally deceased.

"Count me in."

"All right, doll, I'll text you the address. Be there by eight tomorrow. And for the love of John Stamos, try to leave the buttah fingers at home."

Buttah fingers. As in butt-*er* fingers. As in the same fingers that managed to spill a hot football stud's piss.

"Got it."

With a swift end to the call, I headed back to my apartment, and once inside, set my grocery bags on the kitchen counter. I had the milk, eggs, and bread unpacked when I heard the hallway toilet flush.

"You're out of toilet paper!" Abby shouted from the bathroom, the sounds of running water from the sink faucet only slightly muffling her voice.

I'd already known about the toilet paper shortage, hence one of the main reasons I'd made a grocery store run at nine in the morning on a Sunday, but I hadn't known she was here.

But with Abby's track record for unpredictability, this was nothing more than routine, and any surprise at the sound of her voice was limited.

"When did you get here?" I asked out of habit as she walked into the kitchen.

"Last night."

I scrunched up my nose. "What in the hell time?"

"Who knows. Maybe a little after two?"

"Seriously? How did I miss you when I left this morning?"

I knew the question was pointless the instant I'd asked it.

Abby was like a little ninja. She had the power to creep around my apartment without me ever realizing she was here.

I probably should've been more concerned about that reality, but she'd been my best friend for what felt like forever. Plus, the worst she'd do was eat all of my cookies.

"Not sure." She shrugged and started rifling through the grocery bags I'd yet to unpack. "Randy really liked your place, by the way."

"Randy?" I asked and turned to watch as she opened my fresh box of vanilla wafers and started munching on them. "I don't know a Randy."

"I didn't either…." She paused and waggled her brows. "Until last night."

"So, let me get this straight," I started and rested my hip on the kitchen counter. "You brought some strange man back to my apartment, and did what? Had sex on my couch?"

Her appearances were old hat, but I had to admit, the additional detail of using my apartment as some kind of hookup hotel came as a bit of a shock. One I wasn't quite sure I was ready to come to terms with.

And, apparently, I'd been mistaken. The worst she could do was eat all of my cookies *and* have sweaty sex with random dudes on my couch. I offered up a silent prayer they never occurred at the same time.

She shrugged again and popped another wafer into her mouth. "The details are a bit fuzzy, but I think you've got the gist of it."

God. Good thing I'm a sound sleeper.

"Gross."

"Trust me, Randy is not gross," she retorted, completely unfazed by the situation. "He's just a good old-fashioned guido from Jersey. Attractive, maybe a little stupid, and a set of washboard abs I could grate your new package of cheddar cheese on," she said, holding up the cheese as a prop.

"Don't you think you should take your one-night stands back to your place?" I asked far more nonchalantly than I felt. Life with Abby was like life in an alternate universe, and the cyborg version of me was just doing the best she could to navigate it. "I mean, I know that's a huge ask considering I don't even know when you go to your place, but still. It seems like a common courtesy not to defile your best friend's couch."

"Don't worry, sweet cheeks, I'll Lysol the upholstery."

I blinked. Sighed. Resigned myself to the fact that I couldn't take back Abby's fun night with Randy's sweaty balls no matter how hard I tried. "Oh, wow. You're too kind."

Abby winked. "That's what friends are for."

"Besides disinfecting my couch, what are your plans for the day?"

She shrugged. "Not much besides convincing you to make me French toast."

I rolled my eyes. I wished I were bold enough to ask for things like Abby was. It didn't matter whether she'd just stolen your last brownie or not, she could convince anyone of anything. A cop not to give her a ticket. A doorman to let her into a building. A priest that she was, in fact, a devout Catholic who was eligible to take communion during her cousin's christening, and apparently, me, to make her French toast even though she'd just sullied the most expensive piece of furniture in my apartment.

"You know, sometimes I feel like I'm a single mother with a seventeen-year-old daughter."

Abby laughed. "Your daughter is kind of a floozy."

"Tell me about it," I retorted with an involuntary grin. She really had a special kind of charm I couldn't put my finger on. "Guidos named Randy aren't the kind of men I want her hanging around with."

"Don't worry, Mom," Abby joked back. "Randy isn't boyfriend material. He was just a guy I wanted to fuck."

I laughed. "Well, if that isn't music to every mother's ears."

While she made coffee, I turned on the stove and started prepping for my famous French toast. Eggs, milk, butter, bread, and my recipe's secret, a little vanilla and cinnamon.

Once my best friend had her coffee mug filled to the brim, she made herself comfortable on the kitchen counter and watched as I cooked breakfast.

"So," she started after taking a long sip from her mug, "any news on the job front?"

"Mable called me earlier this morning, actually," I said and flipped the bread in the pan. It sizzled, and butter bubbled up around the edges. "I'll be handling packing and shipping for a small store in Brooklyn."

"What kind of store?"

I shrugged. "They either sell stationery or crafts."

"I'd rather gouge my eyes out than do that job."

"Tell me about it," I agreed. "But beggars can't be choosers. The pay is pretty good, and it's a steady job for the next three months."

"Christ, Gem." She snorted, and I looked up at her.

"What?"

"You do realize you've had more random jobs in the past two months than I've had my whole damn life, right?"

"Considering you hardly work and I'm still trying to figure out how you pay your freaking bills, that's not a fair comparison. I know how you afford food, though," I said pointedly and jerked my head toward the box of vanilla wafers—*my box of vanilla wafers*—in her greedy hands.

A smile and a little shrug told me my accusations, true or not, didn't concern her.

I really didn't know how Abby paid her bills. Besides her occasional, pretty much whenever-she-felt-like-working job at a coffee shop called Cool Brew, the girl's ability to pay for anything was a goddamn mystery. And whenever I asked about it, she brushed it off with a simple, "I have a little money saved up."

If I didn't know her penchant for lazy firsthand, I would've thought she was a high-priced hooker. But even Abby Willis, escort extraordinaire, wouldn't keep any damn clients with her laissez-faire approach to work.

"But seriously, Gem, you can't deny you've had *a lot* of jobs." She snorted again and started ticking off my most recent jobs on her fingers. "Dog walker, maid at a bed-and-breakfast, server for a catering company, salon assistant, a receptionist—"

"I get it."

"I'm not even half done. And let's not forget about your one-day stint in piss collection."

Okay. Yeah. So I'd had a decent amount of jobs in the past few months.

The dog walking gig was only temporary, and I had actually been pretty good at it.

The Millers were a rich family in Manhattan and had three adorable corgis named after the Three Stooges. I'd loved those fucking dogs, but sadly, the Millers had relocated to Atlanta and taken my furry friends with them.

Being a maid hadn't been a good match. I mean, I could hardly keep my own apartment clean, much less clean up after other people.

Working at the salon had gone tits up when I'd accidentally re-filled one of the dye bottles with the wrong color. To say Mary Lou had been a little pissed that her hair had turned out far more blond than the auburn glaze she'd been going for would be an understatement. She'd all but threatened my life, and the salon owner had to kindly ask me to leave before her client resorted to actual murder.

And the other jobs? Well, they'd all kind of ended the same way. Clearly, none of them was right for me.

"All right, all right," I said and raised my spatula hand in the air. "So I've had a decent amount of jobs in the past two months."

Abby grinned. "A decent amount? More like a ridiculous amount."

"I just haven't found a good match."

"Because you're in the wrong damn business, honey."

I rolled my eyes. "Not the whole music thing again."

"Yes," she said. "But only because I think you're crazy talented, and it's your secret passion that you haven't realized is actually your soon-to-be career."

I slapped two hot pieces of French toast onto a plate and shoved them toward her. "Just go eat your French toast and stop talking like a crazy person."

She glared as she walked away, all the way to the little kitchenette table I had set up just outside the kitchen.

I loved music, I *really* loved my new guitar, and I might've spent most of my free time writing new songs and finding open mic nights throughout the city.

But it was a hobby.

It didn't pay the bills, and it sure as shit wasn't a career path.

I looked to Abby as her harping ran through my head and careened into the barrier of practicality every time. Even, let's face it, when it came to her. With a pseudo-squatter in my apartment who wouldn't stop eating my food, I needed a steady income to pay the bills.

Hell, from what I could tell, and the frequency of her visits, if I didn't keep up with the rent, we'd both be out of a home.

Okay, so that might've been a bit of an exaggeration, but the cold hard truth remained, paying bills with my music wasn't an option.

I mean, I came from a family of go-getting engineers.

From childhood on, it'd been all but pounded into my head to stay far away from creative jobs like music or writing or photography because they were too unstable and unpredictable to build a secure future.

Mind you, my grandfather called them "artsy-fartsy" jobs. He also adamantly defined them as the opposite of practical or realistic.

And as much as I would've secretly loved for music to be my livelihood, it just wasn't a viable career choice for me.

Chapter Six

Leo

Music pounded from the backyard as I pulled up in the drive behind several expensive cars, shut off the engine, and climbed from my five-year-old Dodge Durango that my parents gave me as a high school graduation present.

It was team bonding time. And the location? Quinn Bailey's backyard.

The first game of the season was this coming weekend, and team cohesiveness, owner Wes Lancaster had insisted, was of the utmost importance. I understood where he was coming from, but all the necessity in the world didn't stop me from feeling a little bit like a fish out of water.

Most of these guys had been under contract with the Mavericks or other big-time teams for years, and the money for a new car or a fancy house was nothing more than a drop in the bucket.

But I was the new guy, fresh out of college with a nice-sized signing bonus but absolutely no guarantees as to how long or how far my ability would take me in a seriously high-stakes sport.

I'd set my bonus aside, in a fund with my financial advisor, just in case when my three years were up, my luck was too.

Don't get me wrong, I was damn good on the field, and I had the drive of four guys combined. But playing in college and playing in the big show were two entirely different things, and I wanted to be smart.

My parents and my Nonna, my dad's aunt, had taught me to be that way.

Checking any nerves and replacing them with the swagger of someone far cockier than I really was, I moved to the gate in the vinyl fence at the side of the house and pushed it open to a crowd of some of the biggest guys in the world.

Six five, six six, 350 pounds, these weren't the kind of people who ever had a shot at being a jockey.

They were big and lean, and most of them had moments of being mean.

Primarily on the field, I presumed, but hell if I knew how they treated the rookies the rest of the time. Besides practice and conditioning, I hadn't spent much time with any of them. In fact, this was the first time I was seeing most of them outside of Mavericks Stadium.

Sean Phillips was the first to spot me as I stepped inside the yard and clicked the gate shut behind me, nudging Cam Mitchell with an elbow to turn around and look for himself.

Normally, I prided myself on being the kind of guy who stood confidently and demanded respect. But I'd already had a couple of run-ins with Cam where all had not gone well. I hadn't been a complete fuckup, but he'd certainly gotten some kicks out of messing with me, and I'd played right into his hands. And, as a teasing smile lit his face at the sight of me, I wasn't sure my embarrassing stint with him was done.

Falling into step together, the two of them headed in my direction, swift and true, and I did everything I could to cover up the fact that I kind of wanted to turn around and leave.

Predators prey on the weak—even the ones big enough to prey on the strong—and being a cocky little shit in front of the two of them was my only form of protection.

I saddled up to enlist the persona's help, crossing my arms over my chest and settling into my spot to make them come all the way to me.

If they were going to give me shit, it was going to be on my terms.

"Well, well, well," Sean said when they arrived. "Look what the cat dragged in, Cam."

"I see," Cam said, pretending to sniff the air. "It stinks. Smells like…" More sniffing. "Newbie."

I cracked a smirk at that and stuck out a bold hand. Sean's eyes dropped to it meaningfully while Cam's grin turned into a smile. Neither moved to take it.

"Interesting start you've had with the team," Sean mused instead, leaning an elbow into Cam's shoulder.

Cam's smile turned mischievous. "I'll say. Messing up the piss test on the first official day as a team member. Has to be some kind of record."

Sean laughed. I grimaced. Two months later and I was still getting shit about the whole pee debacle. It was bad enough that I'd gotten a reaming from Wes Lancaster about messing up the first of my retakes and had to go back for yet a third time—a transaction I completed successfully, by the way—but it was even worse that I hadn't been able to go to a single practice in the time since then without someone cracking a joke at my expense.

It was a huge change from being the most popular guy on my college team, but I was finally getting used to the adjustment. Plus, the amusement associated with my humiliation had to pass at some point. *Right?*

Yeah, thanks for the support, guys.

"Definitely," Sean responded with amusement. "I've never actually heard of that happening, you know? Honest to God, I think you're the first."

I rolled my eyes. "I'm sure I'll be the first for a lot of things around here."

Cam guffawed. "Is that right?"

My chest puffed out involuntarily.

"You bet."

"What do you think, Cam?" Sean said teasingly. "First one to show up to practice in panty hose? Or the first to fail miserably against the big dogs?"

"First one to give you a run for your money and then some," I challenged.

Sean's eyes lit, clearly reveling in the shit-stirring and the news that I was now a willing participant.

One thing was for sure. When you engaged with these guys, you'd better be ready to go the distance. Luckily, I had an extensive background in shit-talking, and all in all, I had the goods to back it up. I was comfortable on the field, and when really necessary, absolutely thrived under the pressure.

"Well, I guess we'll see," Cam remarked, rolling the toothpick in his teeth to the other side of his mouth and grinning. "First game this weekend will settle that."

I nodded. We *would* see at the first game. It would be make it or break it time, and I had everything inside me gearing up for it by the day.

Everything *smart* inside me, that is.

The stupid parts—ironically linked to my dick—were focused on something a little different.

And as it happened, Sean decided to play right into my stupid dick's metaphorical hands.

"So how exactly do you mess up a piss test anyway, Landry? I've been dying to know. Personally, I'm a pro when it comes to handling the one-eyed snake, and honestly, I can't imagine how someone can fuck that up."

He turned to Cam cheekily.

"I mean, what kind of voodoo dance do you have to attempt with your dick to spill the piss everywhere?"

Cam laughed and neglected to answer, but I filled in the gaps. I wasn't sure it made me sound better, to tell the truth, but I was fairly certain it couldn't make me sound worse.

"The medical tech—"

"Cute little blond?" Sean interjected.

I gave a tight nod, hoping the simple motion wouldn't give too much away. "Yes."

"Yeah, I remember her. Spunky little thing."

Spunky little thing. I hated the way those three tiny words rolled off his tongue with ease.

"Aren't you with someone?" I challenged irrationally, and just like that, I'd completely given away my hand. Two fucking months and the memory of her was still driving me crazy.

What the fuck is wrong with me?

"Why yes, yes, I am. How funny that you would notice."

Cam laughed, pointing to Sean with a wag of his finger. "Annnd bring it up."

I rolled my eyes, but they kept on.

"Seems like maybe he's got a crush, Cam."

"Seems extremely likely, Sean."

"You two should take this on the road," I remarked on a shake of my head. "Really."

"Ah, come on, man," Sean said with a laugh. "We're getting to know you. Your likes, dislikes, strengths, weaknesses."

Cam nodded. "So far we know you like blonds, and you're weak as shit at peeing in a cup."

At that, I laughed. A real genuine chuckle at my own expense. And finally, Sean's smile turned from menacing to friendly.

Apparently, self-deprecation was the key to cracking his code.

"Come on, Leo. Let's get a beer and talk a little more."

I, of course, agreed readily. It was one thing to keep myself guarded until I proved my worth, but it was another to reject the idea of bonding with two of the most popular and talented guys on the team. Sean Phillips and Cam Mitchell wouldn't be bad friends to have. Not at all.

Of course, all bad stories start with the good, and this one in particular was the beginning of how I made a decision I wasn't sure I would have without the aid of so much alcohol.

Bottoms up!

Four hours later

While the rest of the party rolled on outside, Cam, Sean, and I sat inside Quinn Bailey's basement and stared at Sean's laptop.

"Trust me," Sean slightly slurred for the ninth time in fifteen minutes as he flashed his agile fingers over the keyboard. "I use this profile for all kinds of shit, and no one has ever traced it back to me."

"How do I know you're not setting me up?" I asked with the expected mental clarity given how drunk I was. Which, yeah, equated to not very much.

"You don't," Cam comforted with a meaty-handed slap to my back. "You're the rookie and you don't know shit, but we know this. Sean's got this. Trust."

His pep talk was about as clear as mud, but somehow, in the moment, it was all I needed to hear. It was steadying and precise and encouraging all at once. Basically, as far as drunk Leo was concerned, drunk Cam was a genius.

Hell, if you'd asked me right then, I would've said Cam was a certified motivational speaker and should take that shit on the road. Oprah, Ellen, TED, the whole fucking shebang.

Clearly, we'd been heavy into the beer and liquor, and it'd be a minor miracle if I made it out of this without a monster fucking hangover tomorrow morning.

But for now, though, I was apparently only suffering from poor judgment.

Sean clicked the final button, and just like that, sent my romantic search into the ether of the internet.

"I'm telling you," he said, just as he and Cam high-fived. "If you can't find this girl with a post like this on Reddit, you can't find her."

I nodded my agreement, timid as it was, and recited the title of the post as it stared back at me.

Help me find the girl who spilled my pee: A desperate plea

I wasn't sure if it was the best idea I'd ever heard or something I'd wholeheartedly regret once the alcohol had found its way out of my system.

But hell, with the way both Cam and Sean had appeared fucking certain of the Reddit game plan since I'd explained the whole mystery girl situation, I couldn't muster any negative emotions toward my big, anonymous debut into online threads.

I mean, who knows, maybe I'll actually find her?

Chapter Seven

Gemma

At five minutes till eight, I pulled into the parking lot of a building that read Marty's Craft Supplies. It matched Mable's rundown of the job in both address and description, so I figured I'd found the right place and hopped out of my car to walk inside.

Truthfully, I couldn't say I'd always been that successful in finding my new jobs on the first shot. I'd walked into the wrong place and argued with employees about how they should have been expecting me, been late thanks to driving in circles, and asked questionable things at a massage place I'd stumbled into while looking for the doggy day spa where I'd been hired to fill in as the shampoo specialist while one of the employees was on maternity leave.

I wasn't always an airhead, but if you've ever heard about people with book smarts lacking in common sense, I was a good piece of real-life substantiation.

Just before I grasped my hand around the handle of the front door, an elderly woman standing off to the side called my name and startled me. "Gemma?" she asked. "Gemma Holden?"

I nodded, too dumbfounded to do anything else, and stepped

away from the door hesitantly. I loved the elderly, especially sweet strangers who wanted to strike up a conversation, but I was so close to being on time for once. I didn't need Aunt Bea to ruin it.

"Well, aren't you a pretty little thing," she said and eyed me up and down. "Christ, what I'd do to have my tits that perky again."

The pint-sized woman appeared to be in her late seventies, hell, maybe even eighties, and her clothes displayed the most outlandish colors I'd ever seen on someone over the age of fifteen.

Neon pink clashed with glowing yellow, and what would have otherwise been simple nude flats were embellished with enough jewels to make Edward from *Twilight* look dim in the light of the sun.

Even her lipstick was the brightest shade of pink I'd ever seen.

Truthfully, I thought they'd stopped selling that shade around the time Madonna started speaking in an English accent in the nineties for no apparent reason, but evidently, I'd been dead wrong.

Finally, it fully registered that I'd never seen this lady in my life, yet she seemed to know me. Maybe it was the owner? Just getting some fresh air outside the store?

"Are you Marty?" I asked, and a raspy laugh escaped her throat.

"Oh no, honey," she said. "I'd rather play bingo with the old church bitches in my neighborhood than sell damn craft supplies like Marty."

Old church bitches. I wasn't sure whether to crack up laughing or feel bad for the Bible-beating broads. Whoever she was, she was funny. Still, I was on a clock, and my new job was waiting. I couldn't risk losing out on thirty bucks an hour just to stand around and shoot the shit with one of the Golden Girls.

"So, uh, if you're not Marty, then…?"

"I'm Alma," she said and held out her hand to shake mine. "Your new boss."

Okay. Had I accidentally done drugs this morning? Because I was officially confused.

"My new boss?" I asked and glanced between her and the store. "But…I was told to come to this address. To this store, in fact…"

I paused and looked up at the store sign again just to make sure I wasn't seeing things.

Marty's Craft Supplies stood out clear as day.

"Yeah, well, it was the only way I could get that old hag Mable to send me some help," she said, as if it actually explained the confusion.

"So, let me get this straight. You're not Marty, and you don't own this store?"

"Correct."

"Yet you're the one who sent in the work request to my temp agency?"

"Honey, I'm not growing any younger here," she said and pursed her bright-pink lips. "If it takes you any longer to understand this situation, I might croak before we actually get any shit done."

She was a feisty old broad, that was for damn sure, but she was also running low on patience. And if she really was my new boss, it'd probably be a good idea to keep said patience from running on empty.

"Mind explaining why you had me meet you here?" I asked, desperate to have at least one unknown answered. "You know, at a shop that isn't, in fact, your shop?"

She shrugged one bony, neon pink-covered shoulder. "It was the only way after the incident last year."

"The incident?"

"It wasn't a big deal, honey." She tossed one apathetic hand into the air. "A minor confusion if anything, but Mable told me I wasn't allowed to hire any more of their employees."

Jesus Christ. What had I gotten myself into? Was it illegal? Did I need to start sharpening my shanks and figuring out ways for Abby to send them to me now?

Part of me was curious as hell and the other part of me was a bit scared, but the largest part of me still wanted the thirty dollars an hour.

I glanced up and down the street then back at Alma. "So, where *is* your shop?"

"Follow me. I'll lead the way," she said and headed in the direction of the side parking lot. When she opened the driver's-side door of a pearl-white Cadillac, I paused.

"Uh… Your shop isn't on this street?"

Tell me it's not in your fucking car…

She shook her head and slid into the driver's seat. "Just get in your car and follow me." The engine of her boat-sized Caddy revved to life, and she shut the door before I could say otherwise.

Feisty *and* demanding, she was a woman on a mission, and not a single person, certainly not me, could stop her.

So I did what any chick needing a paycheck would do; I hopped into my Honda Civic, and I followed her.

Surely, this tiny, bright as the sun woman with enough sarcasm to make Amy Schumer look like a comedic amateur wouldn't lead me toward danger. Blood was red, and red was obviously *not* bright enough to be her color. A slaughterhouse seemed unlikely.

And in the event I turned out to be wrong, I felt like the odds were in my favor if I had to outrun her.

The drive was short and sweet, and for a senior citizen, she had a bit of a lead foot.

She cruised at nearly fifty miles per hour through streets with speed limits of thirty-five, and whenever a stop sign got in her way, she rolled through that fucker without hesitation.

Before I knew it, she pulled her big-ass Caddy into a circular driveway on a cute little street in the suburbs of Long Island. Woodmere, I think the town was called.

The house connected to the driveway was surprisingly big.

Two stories with a stately entrance, it appeared that old Alma here had some money.

Or maybe, when she'd bought the house in 1930, it hadn't been that expensive.

I pulled in behind the Caddy and was out of my Civic and a few feet behind her by the time Alma had shuffled her way up to the porch.

"Uh…is this your house?" I asked, and she nodded as she un-locked the front door.

"You bet your perky tits it is," she said. "Welcome to my humble abode, Gemma."

She pushed open the front door, but I stayed on the porch. I'd been big in my talk about thinking this wasn't a slaughterhouse, but who knew what creepy things lurked inside. None of today had gone as I'd planned.

"I thought we were going to your shop?"

"This is my shop," she retorted.

What?

"Get with the program, honey," she said and waved impatient-ly for me to step inside. "You're acting like we're living in the damn Stone Age. Online retail is where it's at."

I stepped inside—hesitantly, mind you—and instantly the over-whelming smells of potpourri and one too many lemon-scented Yankee Candles filled my nostrils.

She shut the front door behind me and set her purse and keys down on the top of a midcentury-looking divider that separated the entryway from the living room.

Bright orange carpet. Green floral couches. And plastic cover-ings snugly placed over every damn seat in the house.

I might as well have taken a time machine back to 1963.

"Follow me," she said and shuffled down the entryway, through the kitchen where orange appeared to be the theme, and into a back room that had to be the dining room. At least, that was my assump-tion given the table buried under all sorts of things.

"This is where you'll be doing most of your work," she said, pointing toward the table that, after closer inspection, I realized was littered with packages and bubble wrap. "I hope you're a fast learner because I'm behind on about three hundred orders, and there's more coming through every day."

Three hundred orders? Jesus Christ.

"What is it you sell, exactly?"

"Alma's Secrets specializes in pleasure. Toys, lingerie, you name it, and we've got it."

"Toys?" I asked around a choked swallow. "As in sex toys?"

"You got it," she said matter-of-factly. Like it was the most normal thing in the world for a lady of her age to be selling sex goodies online. "I have a main site of my own, but I also sell through Etsy and eBay."

Alma chatted on about sex toys as she rifled through a big cardboard box and started pulling out some of her inventory while I stood silent. *Overwhelmed.*

Dildos.

Vibrators.

Lacy lingerie.

Bottles of numbing lube.

She was literally in the business of pleasure.

She'd run through at least six products and her likes and dislikes about each by the time she noticed I'd clammed up like a mobster in an interrogation room.

"Oh God, don't tell me you're like that last chickadee Mable sent over," she muttered and set a package with the words "The Motherfluffer" written across it onto the dining room table. It took everything I had to form words, and I hadn't understood the question.

"I'm sorry…what did you say?"

Luckily, or very unluckily, depending on how you looked at it, she repeated the question in her blunt version of layman's terms.

"Are you a virgin?"

"Excuse me?" My eyes widened, and my pulse sped up at her audaciousness. "Are you really asking me if I'm a virgin?"

"Well, I kind of have to after the last incident that got me blackballed from Mable's list," she said without any ounce of shame written on her face. "It wasn't my fault she sent the twenty-year-old version of the Virgin Mary to my house to do inventory. How the hell was I supposed to know a simple vibrator would have her praying to Jesus?"

"I'm not a virgin, even though that's definitely not any of your business. But, uh, how long have you been in the...pleasure business?"

"Let's see," she mused, taking a minute to think back through her memories. "I started this up about a year after my Donnie passed away. Actually, it was me and my best friend Rosie's little company, but then she died about a year ago, and now it's just me running the show."

Instantly, my heart clenched in discomfort for her.

"I'm really sorry for your losses."

She waved a hand in the air. "Don't fret on it, honey. When you get to my age, everyone around you starts croaking. I'm just glad it wasn't me."

I wasn't sure whether to laugh at her sarcasm or cry over the loss of her loved ones.

All I could do was nod. One hour with Alma had proved to be one hell of a ride, and for the first time in my life, I actually understood the saying "full of piss and vinegar."

We both stood there for an awkward moment staring down at the dining room table filled with plastic debauchery, waiting for me to make a decision. She could tell I wasn't sold, but she'd done all she planned in the way of convincing. I had to come to the conclusion on my own.

"So...are you staying or going?" she eventually asked as I met her eyes again.

"Well..." I paused for a brief moment as I tried to wrap my brain around what had to be one of the weirdest situations I'd ever found myself in.

Between the fact that she'd been blackballed from the temp agency I worked for, had tricked my boss with a fake store address, and sold a plethora of sex toys online, I wasn't sure what to do.

Hell, I'd pay a lot of money to meet someone who would know what to do.

"I'll be honest, Alma, I'm not quite sure—"

"How much did Mable say I'd pay you?" she asked suddenly, determination shaping her thinning brow.

"Thirty bucks an hour." At the reminder of that, my resolve for my morals got a little bit thinner. But she spoke before I got the chance to.

"How about this… I'll have Marty call Mable and tell her she has to pull the job opportunity because of financial reasons, and then you can come work for me and I'll pay you thirty-five bucks an hour under the table?"

Well, shit. How in the hell was I supposed to say no to that?

Not only was it a five-dollar hourly increase, but she was pretty much giving me the option not to claim it on my taxes.

IRS, if you're reading this, obviously, I'm just kidding.
I claim everything on my taxes.
Please don't audit me.

"Okay." I held out my hand to shake hers. "You've got a deal, Alma."

She grinned. "Fantastic."

I felt a little like I'd sold my soul to the devil. Well, if the devil was an elderly woman sporting bright-pink lipstick and bedazzled Easy Spirits who sold sex toys.

But with Alma running the show, I didn't have time to rethink my decision.

She dove headfirst into work after that, and the rest of the day was a blur of learning the ropes.

Alma showing me the inner workings of her online business. Me trying not to gag when she went into a long ramble about which items were her favorites and explained what do with the return pile.

Come on. Returns? *On sex toys?*

What was wrong with people?

I can understand where some of you may be curious what
happens with the return pile, but I can tell you from real-life
experience, you do not want the answer to that question. So, I'm
going to go ahead and play my trump card here and keep that
traumatic information to myself.

By the time the clock struck three in the afternoon, Alma demanded I take a break from my current task of preparing shipment
labels and have a coffee break with her out on the back terrace.

Alma's version of a back terrace looked a lot like something
MTV's *Cribs* would have featured in its prime. Lush landscaping. A
big-ass pool with a Jacuzzi. Old Alma, nutty as a fruitcake though
might she be, had some serious dough.

"I hope you're not going to take offense to this, Alma, but why
do you even bother with the whole online business thing? I mean, it
appears you're not hurting for money..."

She shrugged and took a sip of her coffee. "For most of my life,
Donnie's career was always the priority. Once he passed, I decided I
wanted to do something for myself."

"What did your husband do?"

"He was a defense attorney turned prosecutor turned judge."

"Wow," I said. "That's quite the career."

It was also safe to say I knew why she saved the sex toy business
for after his death. I can't imagine a judge would have been okay with
that kind of publicity.

"My Donnie was an impressive man. Very smart. Ambitious."

She talked with pride and admiration, and a little part of me
squeezed inside. I loved the affection she had for him, but it made me
think about the way my parents used to talk about me...and the way
they most definitely didn't talk about me now.

Shaking it off and focusing on her, I got back to the conversation.

"How long were you married?"

"Just shy of fifty-two years," she responded nostalgically. "I had
all of the best years of my life with that man."

"Did you guys have any kids?"

"Nope," she said. "We were childless. But all three of my sisters had a boatload of kids, and they were always over here spending time with me and their Uncle Donnie, so I've always kind of felt like I got to experience motherhood. Plus, we never really wanted kids of our own. We were far too selfish and liked to travel too much," she said with a little smile. "What about you, honey?" she asked.

"What about me?"

"You got a special man in your life?"

Hah. Yeah, right.

"Nope. I'm currently a lone wolf."

"Do you want a man in your life?"

"Eventually?" I grinned. "Yeah, I think so. But right now, I'm still trying to figure the whole adult thing out."

"I guess that explains why a pretty thing like you is even bothering with temp work."

I snorted. "Yeah. Pretty much."

"Well, you know, my nephew Leonard is a really nice boy. If you ever want to put yourself out there, just let me know and I'm sure I can set something up."

Her nephew Leonard sounded like a fifty-year-old divorced guy, but I kept that assumption to myself. She obviously had a soft spot for him, and I didn't think my first-day impression would end all that well if I jumped right into insulting family.

"I'll keep that in mind," I said and busied myself with a sip of my coffee.

Even though I'd only known eccentric Alma for all of seven hours, I was pretty certain she was the last person I'd seek assistance from in my quest to find a man.

That'd be almost as bad as letting Abby set me up on a blind date.

Guidos from Jersey and middle-aged divorced dudes weren't exactly my speed.

Now, an incredibly handsome man with the bluest eyes I'd ever seen and the body of a professional football god?

Most definitely.

But it'd been weeks and weeks since I'd seen him, and I'd no doubt been too awkward to make any sort of first impression that revolved around the word good.

In fact, I doubted he remembered me at all.

Chapter Eight

Leo

As the team dispersed from the locker room, I grabbed my bag from the locker behind me and slammed it shut. I had to shuffle some clothes around to make room for the dirty ones—that shit could not touch the clean stuff—and the delay in my exit was apparently all the opening Cam Mitchell needed.

"Not bad for a rookie," he said with a slap to my shoulder, rounding the bench to get in front of me.

I crooked a smile, but he turned serious, and I took notice. Serious hadn't been his MO in the few months I'd really known him, and it certainly hadn't been with me.

He was always busting my balls, giving me shit, or testing me on the field with the help of Sean.

But we'd just played our first game of the season—*a 21-to-14 win over Tampa*—and while it wasn't an all-star performance on my part by any means, I hadn't fucked anything up too badly either. I was counting it as a win. At least, I had been until he'd turned serious.

"What's up?" I asked with nerves I was hoping didn't show.

"Not bad for a first game."

I shrugged, unwilling to get my hopes up that he was actually giving me a compliment. I hadn't really earned it, and his behavior prior definitely hadn't taught me to expect it.

"Look, I'm not washing your balls here. You weren't some fucking star out there, but you were something better. You were a team player, and I gotta tell you, that's a fuck of a lot more important than trying to showboat."

My muscles tensed as I tried to take it all in.

The praise felt nice, but the direction felt better. I could focus my energy a hell of a lot better if I felt reinforced in where I was putting it.

"The guys noticed. That's huge. Don't waste the opportunity."

With a bump of his shoulder, he pushed past me and out the locker room door, and I sank to the bench beside my bag.

My nerves were shot, my adrenaline was through the roof, but I'd just gotten the okay from one of the most important players on this team and the advice I needed not to fuck it up.

Immediately, the first person I always wanted to celebrate with came to mind.

My biggest friend. My greatest champion. My Nonna.

Digging for my phone in the outside pocket of my bag, I pulled it out and typed a quick text.

She was geriatric, but she was forward-thinking, and according to our last FaceTime chat, I was supposed to text her just like one of the "cool kids". Mind you, those were her words, not mine.

I nearly laughed at the memory of her face as she said that to me and typed in her number to hit send.

Me: Hey, Nonna. Just got done with my first game. Wish you could have been here.

Nonna: I watched, don't worry. Of course, if I saw you more often, I might have been able to pick up some tickets and come.

The old biddy knew she could get tickets to a game anytime she wanted, but obviously, my Nonna had a flair for the dramatic.

I chuckled at her near-immediate jump into guilting me and typed out another message.

Me: I know it's been too long. But I've been a little busy, you know. Playing pro football doesn't exactly equate to a plethora of free time.

Nonna: Horseshit. There's always time for your Nonna. I could even do some exercises with you.

Me: That's sweet, but I don't know that exercising with you would be a good enough workout.

Nonna: Are you trying to say I'm not fit? I've been doing them Jane Fonda videos.

Me: Yeah, that's great, but I haven't seen Jane take on a guy who weighs 350 pounds.

Nonna: Oh, she could. Believe you me. Jane can take on anyone with her goddamn thighs alone.

I grimaced at the visual and raised the white flag via text.

Me: Okay, Nonna. Whatever you say. I'll have to take your word for it.

Nonna: You should take all my words. And I'd be happy to give them to you at lunch next week.

Me: Subtle, Nonna.

Nonna: Subtle is for schoolgirls and priests, and I'm neither of those. I'll see you next week. Maybe that'll stop my beloved sister Darla from rolling over in her grave.

I laughed at the timely mention of my dead grandmother and admired my Nonna's spunk. It was one of the reasons I loved her most, and the number one reason I didn't want to think about her not being around one day. It also made it easy to feel bad about not seeing her, even when she wasn't slathering on a thick coating of guilt. With my parents' recent relocation to Florida, she was the only local family I had left.

Me: Okay. I'll try to make lunch one day next week work.

Nonna: I'll see you then.

Me: I said I'd try.

Nonna: Wednesday at noon works good for me too.

Me: Nonna…

Nonna: Bye now. Love you, dear.

My laughter echoed through the locker room as I shook my head. Man, she was a pistol.

Me: I'll let you know.

Nonna: Dress nice. I want you to meet someone.

Me: Nonna.

Nonna: What's that, dear? I don't understand.

Me: I said one word, and it was your name.

Nonna: These texts are breaking up.

Me: That's not a thing. Texts don't break up like calls.

Nonna: Static, dear. Just static.

Me: I know you can see what I'm writing.

Nonna: Better hang up now.

Me: You can't hang up a text!

Nonna: Oh, well. Just did. See you Wednesday. And good job at the game. You had the cutest butt out there.

God, she was relentless. And I couldn't imagine I could love anyone more.

But the idea of meeting someone—someone I knew would be female and a setup of a romantic nature—didn't appeal even a little.

I still couldn't get the mystery girl out of my head. At this point, I wasn't sure I ever would.

With that thought in mind, I did what I seemed to do almost every time I had my phone in my hand anymore—I went directly to Reddit, hoping that someone had found the woman who spilled my pee.

I scrolled and scrolled through the most recent comments.

Some chuckled it up over my request. Which, I couldn't deny, from an outsider looking in was a trippy as fuck post.

Some people posted their own versions of similar situations.

And others just wished me the best.

But other than that, so far, no luck.

Mystery girl was still just that—a fucking mystery.

Chapter Nine

Gemma

One week into working for Alma Waters, and it was still a bit of a shitshow.

I'd officially started working for her outside of the temp agency's jurisdiction, and I'd even turned down another job Mable had offered when this one "fell through."

Mable had been a bit confused when my money-hungry self had actually said no to a job, but I'd played it off by telling her I was temporarily helping out my dad and grandfather with administrative work at their consulting firm.

And, yeah, even though I'd most likely bitten off more than I could chew, I had no other choice than to swallow fast and get on with it.

Day two of working for Alma included a drive to a nearby park where we took photographs of the new inventory. Why had she felt it was best to do it in a park? Well, because Alma says nature is the perfect conduit for pleasure. Whatever the fuck that means.

The photo shoot had generated quite the curiosity from passers-by, and when Alma wanted to take pictures of silk lingerie dangling from a tree branch, I'd turned redder than a beet in its prime.

Days three and four had revolved around speed-packing and packaging more vibrators than I could count.

And day five had involved me going to the post office with Alma in tow. Which I quickly understood was a big fat mistake when she'd attempted to keep the shipping costs down by telling the guy behind the counter everything fell under media mail.

Media mail, for those of you who are unaware, is cheap postage for books, CDs, and DVDs.
Sex toys and lingerie, on the other hand?
Not even fucking close to media mail.

Needless to say, the post office guy wasn't born yesterday and called bullshit.

But to my—*and pretty much everyone else in the post office's*—surprise, after fifteen minutes of Alma arguing that *pleasure items* are not treated fairly, he gave her some kind of employee discount.

I think it was more out of fear she'd start a Sex Toys Equal Rights rally right there in the lobby than anything else.

With the way she'd been smiling like a loon as we'd left the post office, it was pretty obvious that wasn't the first time she'd argued her way into a deal.

Obviously, at just a week into the madness, this was only the beginning. I wondered if, over time, I'd become desensitized to all of it or if the trauma would just build and build until I had to spend all of my hard-earned money on a therapist.

I guessed only time would tell.

"Honey, you need to use a lot more bubble wrap when you're packaging the larger dildos," Alma instructed from her perch at the other end of the dining room table. "We have to make sure they get to where they're going intact."

I was four hours into day seven of the job, and already, Alma had a lot to say.

I, on the other hand, had been startlingly silent. The dildo in question was bigger than my forearm, and words felt unthinkable while the urge to cover my vagina with my hand was so strong.

When the shock wore off, curiosity took over. Holding it up in the air, I asked, "People actually use these things?"

"There's nothing wrong with wanting a big cock, sweetie."

Big cock. The words fell straight from her lips as if she'd said "sweet tea."

"Yeah, I get that, Alma, I really do," I said, and my nose scrunched up in disagreement. "But I don't see how anyone could use this thing without causing internal damage. Aren't you worried someone's going to send you their ER bill after they give this mighty beast a go?"

"Don't worry," she said and took a sip from her morning coffee. "Anything that we sell has been tested and certified."

"Tested?" I questioned with wide eyes and thanked Jesus himself that there wasn't more to my job description. "Who in their right mind would be willing to test—" I glanced down at the package in my hands and read the label out loud "—'King Dong Dildo'?"

Alma looked at me.

And I looked at Alma, and just before she opened her mouth to respond, I regretted asking the question.

"I test all of my own products," she said.

"You test all of your own products?"

"Of course I do." She looked at me like I was the crazy person out of the two of us. "What kind of business owner would I be if I couldn't back my own products?"

There it was. I had my answer. Desensitization was impossible. It would take years and years of therapy for me to get past the trauma that had just left her lips and reached my ears.

Not that I thought little old Alma should be some kind of celibate nun, but for the love of God, I didn't want to know the ins and outs of her sexual health.

Moving right along and ignoring the entire conversation that had quite possibly caused future brain damage, I hopped up from my chair and grabbed some extra bubble wrap from Alma's garage.

Once I found what I needed, I went back inside and proceeded to pack up about fifteen King Dong Dildos, all the while I offered up a silent prayer for every single recipient.

Please, Jesus, keep Mindy Franklin's lady bits safe. And when Sue Crosby gets this package in the mail, please encourage her to read the safety instructions prior to use.

In the name of the Father, Son, and the Holy Spirit, Amen.

By the time King Dong was all packed up and ready to ship out to its next victims, I headed into Alma's kitchen to make a fresh cup of coffee.

"You need another cup?" I called toward the dining room.

"No thanks, honey," she responded. "Too much coffee will end up giving me the shits."

"Well, by all means, the last thing we want is for you to get the shits," I teased, and she just laughed.

"Tell me about it. I went to Applebee's with the girls last week for dinner, and after eating a basket of boneless wings, I spent my night on the pot, farting up a storm."

Thank you for that lovely tidbit of terrifying information, Alma.

I grimaced as I added sugar and creamer into my cup.

"You like boneless wings, Gemma?"

If she would've asked me yesterday, I would've said hell yes, but now, after she'd tainted them with her intestinal commentary, I wasn't exactly craving a happy hour at Applebee's. Or anywhere with wings, for that matter.

Buffalo Wild Wings, Wings and Rings, you name it, and she'd ruined it.

"They're okay."

"Personally, I'm a mild wings kind of gal," she added as I walked back into the dining room and sat down. "I think that's why I had the shits the other night. I went for the medium, thinking I could handle the spice."

Are we really still talking about wings and Alma's bowels?

"So, uh, what's next on the agenda?" I asked by way of changing the conversation to something that wouldn't ruin my appetite.

"Did you get all of the King Dong Dildos packaged up?"

"Yep," I responded like it wasn't weird at all for an elderly woman to say the words Dong or Dildo. "I figured I'd leave a little earlier today and drop them off at the post office before I head home."

"Make sure you tell him its media mail."

I wanted to laugh at her determination. "Alma, with all due respect, those big-ass packages aren't going to cut it as media mail."

"You don't think so?"

"Uh…no…I know so," I said and couldn't stop myself from laughing. "I understand your creative attempts to thwart the system, but sweet Jesus, you're going to have to pick something a little less monstrous to do it with. If anything, those insanely huge items will need extra shipping just to get them where they need to go."

She smirked. "They are pretty big, huh?"

"Alma, they should come with a complimentary prayer card and an ice pack."

"I'll make note of that for future sales." A soft, raspy laugh left her lungs. "And the next thing I really need you to help me with today includes moving some of the newest inventory from the garage into the dining room."

I followed her lead toward the garage, but just before we stepped through the door, she paused and pointed toward a wooden-framed photograph hanging on the wall. "That's my nephew Leonard I was telling you about."

With braces, an awkward smile, and a bowl cut, old Leonard looked to be about twelve or thirteen in the photo.

Alma smiled lovingly at his photo. "Isn't he handsome?"

Handsome was a bit of a stretch for this photo, but in eighth-grade Leonard's defense, no one, no matter who the hell they were, looked good at that age. I moved my eyes away before I could criticize his most awkward years too thoroughly.

Hell, I was pretty certain my school photo from that time included crimped hair, blue eye shadow, and acne.

"Very handsome," I lied.

"You know, you should meet my Leonard," she said with a smile. "He's a bit of a cocky shit, but as you can see, he's a real looker."

Even though I'd yet to see the real-life Leonard, and all I had to go by was his stuffy name and eighth-grade picture, I kind of felt like calling him a real looker might have been a bit of a stretch.

But I kept my bitchy thoughts to myself and just hummed in agreement. The best defense to a setup was always quiet contemplation.

My parents had been shoving prospects my way for years, and they only got really pushy when I rejected the idea outright. I had to assume Alma would be the same way.

Eventually, she'd forget about dreams of me and Leonard.

And maybe one day, I'd be able to forget about her and King Dong.

Chapter Ten

Leo

Ten seconds on the clock—ten seconds away from winning our second game of the season—and I could feel the sweat dripping down my back. The Miami heat was a change of pace from New Jersey's slow fade into fall, and the adrenaline of maybe playing a part in maintaining a winning season as a rookie was at an all-time high.

Miami's quarterback grunted the call, loud and gravelly as always, and all of us tensed in our positions. With a clap and a stomp of his toe, he shouted for their center to snap the ball and send it spiraling back for his waiting hands.

I dug my cleat into the turf and took off at a sprint, running my coverage of one of their best receivers with as much speed and precision as I could manage.

My heart pounded, my palms sweated, and time slowed to a crawl.

The ball spiraled toward us, a prediction I'd have made any day of the week given the prowess of Edwards, Miami's all-star receiver, and I churned my legs to keep up with his moves and then some.

Reading the line of the pass, I juked and turned, spinning to the back and jumping up in front of Edwards in a streak of luck and skill.

I stretched, reaching to my full height and beyond as the skin of the ball met my fingertips and struggled to sail straight through.

But I wouldn't be stopped—not this time—gritting my teeth into the cushion of my mouthguard and clamping my fingertips with the strength of twenty men.

The ball secure, I fell to my feet and, with assistance from Edwards, continued straight to the ground in a heap with 270 pounds of angry muscle on top of me.

But I had the ball in my hands and could feel the roar of excitement all around me.

Miami's drive had officially been stopped, the game was over, another tally in the win column in our favor, and I'd been the one to make the game-ending play.

Climbing to my feet, I basked in the moment…

For about a second before the team was upon me and I was back on the ground.

Holy fuck, did it feel good.

"Hell yeah!" Cam yelled, smacking me on the helmet and getting right in my face. The rest of the pile hooted and cheered and shifted until, finally, Quinn Bailey took it upon himself to dig me back out.

With a helping hand, he dragged me to my feet and smacked me on the helmet three times before bringing our heads together.

"That's what I'm talking about, Landry!" he shouted over the booming and echoing noise in the stadium.

Miami fans booed and groused, but a fair number of New York diehards could be heard in their midst.

"Mavericks, Mavericks, Mavericks!" they chanted.

"You better get ready, son," Sean Phillips shoved in to announce. "We're gonna party tonight!"

A smile curved the line of my mouth, and I settled into happiness.

Life on the Mavericks was good.

Beer flowing and excitement in the air, the bar where we found ourselves a couple of hours later was the craziest I'd ever seen one.

Somehow, we'd managed to find a colony of Mavericks fans in downtown Miami, and Sean Phillips was hamming it up with every single one of them.

Quinn Bailey had found a quiet spot, tucked in the corner, and Cam Mitchell hadn't left my side once, a meaty arm draped around my shoulder.

I was more than happy to have Cam's devotion, but truthfully, I wasn't sure I wouldn't rather have been tucked away with Quinn.

"This guy here," Cam touted to the crowd. "He's the real deal!"

I rolled my eyes at his theatrics and swayed to his rhythm as the excitement of a new song made him bust out in a dance.

"We Are Family" was fired up on the sound system, and the guys started singing like a pack of lunatics. I laughed and nodded, forgoing participation in actually singing along, and met the eyes of Quinn Bailey in the corner.

He shook his head and tipped his beer to his lips before pulling his phone from his pocket and getting distracted.

Shit. I don't think I remembered to turn my phone back on ring.

Reminded of the contact with the real world I'd been cut off from for the last several hours, I dug my phone from my pocket and lit up the screen.

I had four missed calls, including my parents and a couple of college buddies who were no doubt calling to congratulate me on the win, and several messages from my Nonna.

"I gotta piss," I said as an excuse as I looked up into the glowing face of my Cam Mitchell limb.

He laughed with a smile and shook me back and forth before winking. "Make sure you hit the bowl," he teased.

I flipped him the bird and spun out from under his arm to a chorus of laughter from a bunch of guys and slipped down the hall to the bathroom.

Cloaked in the dark, I stepped off to the side and scrolled through my messages.

Nonna: If I hadn't been boycotting watching the game, I might be inclined to say congratulations.

Nonna: But I am, so I didn't see it. So no congratulations for you.

Nonna: Honestly, I might not live to see another game.

I laughed at her guilt trip and nonsense and typed out another message. Obviously, I'd missed the lunch she'd insisted on the week prior, and if ever there was a woman to hold a grudge, it was my Nonna. She was wicked and twisted, and I loved her more than just about anyone.

Me: Clearly, you saw the game. And clearly, you're proud of me. You don't even have to say it.

Nonna: I'd be proud of someone I saw more than once in a blue moon. You, I barely even recognize. It might not even have been you on the TV. I can't tell anymore.

Me: You know me. And I'm sorry I couldn't come this week, but we had to leave on Wednesday to get down here for pregame stuff.

Nonna: You should have rescheduled to Tuesday, then.

Me: I had practice.

Nonna: Horseshit.

Loud and rich, my guffaw could probably be heard above the blasting music and players.

Me: I'll shoot for this week.

Nonna: I'll start talking to you again when you show up.

Me: I love you, Nonna.

I tried to sweeten her up with kind words and sentiments, but she was just as cutthroat as ever.

Nonna: Whatever.

I sent my mom and dad a quick text letting them know I'd call them tomorrow and resigned myself to contact my college buddies when I made my way back to Jersey.

Before I tucked my phone back into my pocket, I opened my browser and stumbled over to the site I always found myself on once again.

Reddit.

And still, despite viral sharing and tons of fucking comments, the facts were the same.

My mystery girl was still a mystery.

Disappointment hit me square in the chest, but I squashed it down. It didn't matter if I felt up to the hoopla of tonight or not.

It was a rite of passage, and I needed to live in the moment.

I was the man of the hour.

The rookie of the game. And no mystery girl, blond goddess or not, was worth not living in the moment.

There'd be plenty of time to think of her later.

And I would.

Of that, I was certain.

Chapter Eleven

Gemma

"**G**emma, honey!" Alma called from the kitchen. "My nephew Leonard will be stopping by for lunch a little later. So, if you don't mind, try to spruce up the dining room table so we've got somewhere to eat."

"Oh, okay," I said as I finished taping shut a freshly packed box. I figured I'd head to the post office and grab a bite to eat somewhere that didn't require my ass to sit on plastic-covered furniture, and Alma and her nephew would have the time and space to catch up.

Surely, they didn't need me being a third wheel.

And, if I was being honest, I really, *really* didn't want to come face-to-face with the guy Alma kept passively trying to get me to date.

I booked it through the information input process, weighing the package, checking for sizing and shipping method, and selecting the intended shipping date. I wasn't breaking any land-speed records, but I was literally going as fast as I could.

But it was all for naught. By the time I'd printed out the shipping label and attached the damn thing to the box, the doorbell chimed.

"Looks like our special guest has arrived!" Alma singsonged and shuffled her slipper-covered feet into the entryway.

The old bat had said he'd be here a little *later*. But, hot damn, if it'd been all of five minutes since she'd dropped the lunch bomb on me.

So much for making a discreet getaway. I hadn't even had time to clean up!

"Well, well, well…" Her voice echoed off the walls and into the dining room. "It's about time you paid your dear old aunt a visit."

Panic took hold. Alma was maternal in a really twisted way, but she didn't like when she asked you to do something and you didn't get it done. Even if the demand-to-time ratio was ridiculous. Instead of carefully organizing the shit on the dining table, I grabbed an empty cardboard box and shoved everything I could fit inside of it until it was full.

I repeated that cycle two more times before all that was left on the table was a handful of already packed envelopes and Alma's laptop.

No King Dongs or Motherfluffers or Fleshlights in sight, I sighed in relief. Who knew if good old Leonard knew about his aunt's pleasure business, but I sure as hell refused to be the bearer of disturbing-dildo news.

Their muffled voices started to get closer, and I did my best to make myself scarce.

I grabbed Alma's laptop, with the mind-set that I could at least finish organizing my shipping labels, and went into the small sitting room off the formal living room and stayed quiet as a mouse.

Maybe Alma will forget I'm here?

Hah. You wish *she was that senile,* my subconscious taunted.

"Gemma!" Alma called out. "Where are you? I have someone I want you to meet!"

Shit.

"I'm in the sitting room!" I called back. "Just finishing up some invent—" I started to excuse myself, but the old bat was way quicker with her wit than she was with her feet, and I had a feeling she'd known where I was all along.

Alma and her nephew walked into the sitting room, and I'll be damned if I didn't choke on my own tongue.

Familiar, haunting blue eyes.

Chiseled jaw.

Memorable body.

Holy cannoli. It was *the* guy.

Leo "I spilled his pee on myself" Landry.

"Gemma, this is my great-nephew, Leonard," she said, a proud smile permanently etched across her hot pink-colored lips. "Leonard, this is Gemma, my newest *and* favorite employee for my…uh…on-line shop."

Newest and favorite employee? I was her only goddamn employee.

And *great*-nephew? That clarification would've been nice a week ago.

Sweet Lucifer, I didn't know how to react to any of it.

So, I did what I seemed to do best.

I opened my mouth and let words fly out unchecked.

"Uh, hi!" I all but shouted as I hopped to my feet, and my voice echoed awkwardly off the windows of Alma's sitting room. "Hi, Leonard!"

Seriously, you can stop saying hi anytime now…

Good God, obviously, I had no idea what to do.

Do I act like I know him?

Does he even remember me?

How in the hell was I supposed to handle a situation like this?

Just play it cool, Gemma.

"It's…uh…nice to meet you!" I said far too enthusiastically and held out my hand like I was brokering a goddamn business deal. "I'm Gemma!"

So much for playing it cool.

He smirked and took my proffered hand. "It's nice to *finally* meet you, Gemma."

The way his blue eyes sparkled and shone with recognition and his full mouth crested into a knowing smirk, it was apparent Leo Landry knew exactly who I was.

I was *that* girl.

The "I'm so sorry I spilled your pee on myself" girl.

What were the fucking odds I'd ever have to face *that* guy again?

I kind of felt like the universe was trying to shove her boot up my ass.

Here, Gemma, the universe whispered. *I'm going to make you experience one of the most humiliating moments of your life with a really fucking gorgeous man and just a simple specimen cup filled with urine. And then, I'm going to make sure that guy reappears, and then you get to relive it. Isn't that nice?*

No, universe, you conniving little biotch. It wasn't nice at all.

But Leo Landry? Yeah. He looked just as good, if not better, than the first day I'd laid eyes on him.

And this time, I had my doubts a golden shower was the kind of thing that would get me fired. Around here, it might just get me a promotion.

Chapter Twelve

Leo

G*emma.*

Mystery girl from going on two months ago, girl who'd driven me to the brink of crazy thinking about her, girl I never thought I'd find.

Fucking *Gemma.*

And of all places, I'd found her at my Nonna's house, working as her newest employee. And the fact that my dear old aunt needed employees for whatever zany online business store she ran was frankly shocking news, but beggars couldn't be choosers.

Gemma was here, and that was pretty much all I cared about.

In an impressive feat of contortionism, I could practically feel my foot kicking me in the ass as I stood there.

If I'd come earlier. If I'd made lunch work the week before…that would have been a week fewer of suffering.

Good thing I was too fucking thrilled at the sight of her to spend any real time on self-deprecation.

That would come later, I was sure, but something way more important came now.

Gemma.

I took her extended hand in mine and squeezed as warmth ran all the way up the length of my arm. "It's nice to *finally* meet you, Gemma."

She blushed, no doubt still embarrassed by the way we'd met, and I pictured that blush spreading all over her petite body.

God, the fantasies I'd had over the past weeks had nothing on the ones I was conjuring up now, and I knew it was because she looked even fucking better than I'd remembered her.

Blond, petite, adorably dimpled cheeks.

But my God, her eyes were some of the most striking blue beauties I'd ever seen, and the line of her shy smile was enough to make me go weak in the knees.

"You're even better than I remember," I said aloud, totally losing all sense of cool.

She flushed again, pulling her hand from mine on a startle and looking to the ground, just as my Nonna came grumbling into the middle of us. Apparently, she'd missed the weird meeting between us completely.

"Now that the pleasantries are out of the way," she said, "let's get to eating. I'm starving, and the two of you can make moony eyes at the table."

Orrrr not.

Shit.

Panic grabbed Gemma, it was clear to see, as she backpedaled toward the front of the room and a few steps closer to the front door.

I stepped with her, scared I'd have to make a bid to grab her if she made a run for it.

I felt like a crazy person even considering the idea of keeping her here against her will, but Christ, I'd been looking for her without success for almost three months.

I didn't know what I'd do if she just took off again without giving me any real information.

Of course, my Nonna was cruel and unusual, and sometimes, too astute for everyone's good.

She glanced up to see Gemma's moves and called her out on it. "Where are you going?"

Gemma stumbled to come up with an excuse. "Well, see, I forgot I have a dentist appoint—"

"Nope," my great-aunt Alma cut her off. "Next."

Gemma's eyes widened almost comically.

"No, really, I have to—"

"Sit down."

"No, I have to—"

"Get the rolls for me, would you, dear?"

I couldn't hide my smile as Gemma gave in to the power of Nonna, her shoulders sinking slightly in defeat.

I'd been on the other side of this rundown many a time, but somehow, it was a lot more amusing from this sideline.

In fact, I could kind of see why my Nonna seemed to like doing it so much.

"Don't worry," I told Gemma softly as she finally made her feet move and my great-aunt disappeared into the kitchen. "You'll get used to her."

She looked to the carpet and back up again before gracing me with a small smile and a laugh. "I don't know about that. I mean, I've been working here for a little while now, and I've yet to really feel prepared, if you know I mean."

Working for her a little while now? Who would've thought selling T-shirts online would require my eighty-year-old Nonna to turn entrepreneur and start hiring employees?

Certainly not me.

But in my and my family's defense, ever since Great-Uncle Donnie passed away a few years back, no one could really predict what dear old Nonna had up her sleeve.

The old biddy was a fucking wild card, that was for sure, but despite her important presence in my life, in that moment, she wasn't my main focus.

I smiled at Gemma, nodded knowingly, and admitted the truth.

"Yeah. Okay. So you probably won't get used to her," I said through a soft snicker. "Lord knows, I've known her my whole life and never have. But you'll never be short on laughs."

Her pretty blue eyes lit up with amusement. "That much I know. I don't think a day goes by here that I don't laugh."

I looked to the kitchen and back again, and when I met Gemma's eyes once more, they'd changed—warmed.

"She's the best."

With a quick lick of her lips, Gemma gained control of all of the wild emotions cascading through her body. And in the same moment, I lost every bit of control I had.

Good God, I was in trouble when it came to her.

Weeks of not seeing her, minutes of confirming my feelings, and a simple movement—all enough to impact me for a lifetime.

With a gallant hand, I offered her the space to walk into the kitchen ahead of me, and thankfully, she tucked her head and did so.

I adjusted the hard length of my cock behind her, already throbbing beneath my zipper, and fell in line.

By the time I made it to the kitchen, Gemma had acquired the rolls and taken a seat on one side of the table, leaving me the only empty one on the other side.

I rounded the table and pulled out the chair with ease.

At least if I was sitting, I wouldn't have to worry about my body's uncontrollable reactions being exposed.

Nonna reached for my hand and Gemma's and made a stern face to indicate we should close off the circle.

Gemma was hesitant, so I held out an innocent hand, palm up, giving her the space to get comfortable.

Nonna wasn't as generous.

"Are you going to take his hand anytime this century? I'm starving, and the Lord needs his thanks before I can rectify that."

I smothered a smile as Gemma dropped her hand into mine, and I tucked my thumb around the back of it swiftly.

Her hand felt right there, small and delicate in the middle of my large one, and my stomach turned over at the seemingly disproportionate reaction of my heart. It was just holding hands, for shit's sake.

Nonna dove right in. "Dear God Almighty, thank you for this grub. Thank you for directing Leonard into the arms of his dear aunt again, and for sending me a gem like Gemma. Just work on the timing next time."

Gemma's lips sucked in on themselves, and I had to disguise my laugh as a cough.

Only my Nonna could get away with including *direction* for God in the middle of one of her prayers.

"In the name of food and Jesus," she finished, "Amen."

As I dug into the food and gave Gemma the space to freak out, I said a little prayer of my own in my head.

Dear God, thank you for coincidences. And for direct access to a blond I can't seem to get enough of.

Today, I would let her off the hook. But now that I knew where to find her, all bets on the rest were off.

First order of business: shut down that Reddit article for good.

Second order of business: ask Gemma on a date, and don't take no for an answer.

Chapter Thirteen

Gemma

After an awkward *and* completely surprising lunch at Alma's house, I stopped by my parents' for a quick chat and some pie.

For one, I needed the distraction from the fact that I was still trying to wrap my mind around the weird circumstances that kept bringing Mr. Sexy Football Star and me together.

And two, well, my mom had texted and called me no less than six times in the past week, and apparently, the family reunion between Alma and Leonard was inspiring enough to make me do something about it.

Unfortunately, that's where the resemblances stopped. While Leo "Leonard" Landry and Alma had quickly moved from guilt over time and distance to jokes and affection, my family had only gotten colder by the minute. Any time spent here today would apparently be interrogatory rather than quality.

And the lead time hadn't been great either. I'd hardly eaten three bites of my mom's apple pie before Grandpa Joe started in on me.

"All right, I'll be the first one to say it," Grandpa Joe announced. "When are you going to cut the crap, Gemma, and finish your degree?"

My mother sighed.

My dad nodded in agreement.

And me? Well, I kind of felt like flipping my granddad off, but I knew that wouldn't exactly help paint the picture that I was a responsible adult. The whole "you need to finish your degree" conversation had been nonstop since I'd let my family know I'd dropped out of school, and it wouldn't end until I did something to change it.

Working for Alma packaging pleasure goods wasn't exactly the answer. And neither was flipping the bird.

For now, I'd just have to take their questions and bear them.

"I'm not sure." I shrugged and picked at a few rogue apples on my plate. "I left school for a reason. Going back now doesn't make sense."

"It's a bullshit reason, if you ask me," he muttered, and my mother sighed again.

"Grandpa Joe!" she whisper-yelled, actually standing up for me for once. "I think you're being a little hard on her."

"I'm giving her the kick in the ass she needs," he retorted.

"Grandpa, I love you, I really do," I interjected, "but I think it's about time you realize being an engineer is yours and Dad's dream, not mine."

He pursed his lips. "Careers aren't goddamn dreams, Gemma. They're careers. They're supposed to be practical and pay a good wage. Not achieve some crazy fantasy."

"Gemma, your grandpa's right," my dad chimed in. "You can't live paycheck to paycheck doing temp work for the rest of your life. You need to start thinking about your future. Maybe we'd be a little more lenient if you'd actually point yourself in a direction and do something real with your life instead of wandering around like a vagabond."

"I *am* thinking about my future," I said through gritted teeth. For fuck's sake, when would they ever let up on this? The whole reason I'd dropped out of school was because I was *finally* looking at my future. I didn't know what it was, but I was trying to figure it out. I wasn't lazing around on my couch like a bum, and I wasn't pursuing something they'd think was crazy, even if it was something that, deep down, I really wanted to do.

Like music.

What more did they want from me?

"Look," my dad continued. "I know that being an engineer isn't the most exciting job, but it will give you security, sweetheart. And that's all we want for you. We just want to know that you're secure."

"I understand that, but this is my life we're talking about here," I retorted. "And, with all due respect, what I choose is my decision, not yours."

My grandpa hummed his disagreement, and my dad sighed.

The men in my life were not the least bit happy with my choices, but hell's bells, I couldn't live my life for other people. I had to live it for myself.

I think I'd more than proven I could handle my own shit. Sure, my temp jobs weren't anything to write home about, but they paid my bills.

And I sure as shit wasn't running to my parents or Grandpa Joe for money.

I was handling it, albeit slightly messy and unorganized, but handling it all the same.

Appetite successfully gone, I took one small bite of pie and stood up from the table to set my dish in the sink.

Thankfully, my mom led the conversation to less stressful areas and started chatting happily about my dad's and her vacation plans.

Which was great, but I knew time was a ticking.

Eventually, someone would lead that shit right back to me.

By the time Grandpa Joe started bitching about his new land-scaper, I offered my goodbyes with a kiss to my dad's and grand-dad's cheek and a warm hug for my mom, and I headed back to my apartment.

I'd just barely stepped inside my front door when my phone chimed with a text message.

Unknown: Hey, it's Leo.

Leo? As in the guy whose pee I knew on a personal level? As in Alma's nephew? As in Leo Landry? As in the man I'd just spent two of the most awkward hours of my life having lunch with?

No way.

Me: Leo who?

Unknown: Leo Landry.

Unknown: And here I thought I was a little more memorable than that…

Me: LOL. Trust me, considering the circumstances we've found ourselves in, you're memorable. I'm just a little surprised you're texting me. How'd you get my number?

Unknown: Let's just say I know a guy… ;)

I giggled to myself and typed out a response.

Me: You mean you know Alma.

Unknown: Or that too.

"Who are you texting?" Abby asked from the couch, and I damn near bobbled my phone out of my hands.

"Oh my God! You scared the crap out of me!" I leaned against the closed front door and put a hand to my chest. "How long have you been sitting there?"

She nodded toward my face. "Longer than you've been home. And way long enough to see you giggling and smiling like a total weirdo."

"I am not."

"You so are." She grinned. "Who are you texting?"

"You don't know him."

"I didn't ask if I knew him. I asked who he is."

"Leo."

She quirked an eyebrow and then freaked me out with the strength of her memory. "The hot football player from the piss test?"

"Yeah. Him," I said quickly before she could start tossing out quippy lines about shit I didn't want to hear. "Well, you're never going to believe this, but you know that old lady I work for now?"

"The one who likes dildos?"

"She *sells* them, Abby," I corrected.

"Pretty sure she likes them too," she said with a grin, and I rolled my eyes. The last thing I needed was visuals of Alma and King Dongs, but Abby'd officially opened up the dam on painfully uncomfortable memories.

"Anyway...she is Leo's great-aunt."

"Seriously?" Her eyes widened as she kicked her legs up on my couch, crossed her ankles, and put her hands behind her head. "He's the nephew she was low-key trying to set you up with?"

"Uh-huh."

"Fuck." She smirked. "I didn't see that coming."

Yeah, my sentiments exactly.

Startling me so much I jumped, my phone vibrated in my hands. Once I'd started talking to Abby, I'd almost completely forgotten I was *in the middle* of a conversation with Luscious Leo.

Unknown: So...I know we've had a bit of a rocky start in terms of introductions, but I want to start fresh. Are you free tomorrow night?

Me: Free? Are you asking me out on a date, Leonard?

Unknown: I am. And now I'm also asking that you never speak

my full name again.

Me: LOL. In some weird way, I think it kind of suits you.

Unknown: That's the name of a middle-aged man who drives a minivan.

Bingo. That had been *exactly* what I'd pictured when Alma had first told me about her nephew. In a rare moment of boldness, I told Leo just that.

Me: You want to know a secret?

Unknown: Of course.

Me: When Alma told me about her "nephew Leonard," I thought you were a fifty-year-old divorcée with a toupee.

Unknown: Fucking hell.

Me: LOL.

Unknown: Horrible first names aside, will you go on a date with me tomorrow night, Gemma?

Me: That depends.

Unknown: On what?

Truthfully? It depended on whether or not I could stop being such a scaredy cat or not. Not wanting to admit that to him, I made up a question that didn't really matter.

Me: What kind of date did you have in mind?

Unknown: Honestly? I hadn't thought that far ahead. I was too focused on simply getting you to say yes.

"I know the perfect place for you guys," Abby said, and I looked up to find her no longer on the couch, but standing beside me and reading my text messages.

Jesus, she was like a little ninja.

Instantly, I snatched my phone away from her eyes. "You really don't understand personal boundaries, do you?"

She ignored my question entirely. "Seriously, I know the perfect place for you guys. Great food, great music, and hands down, the *best* place for a first date."

Anything from Abby made me skeptical, but I needed the help. If I didn't offer up her suggestion, I wouldn't have anything else to say.

With a wing and a prayer, I offered myself up to the Abby gods.

Me: How about you pick me up tomorrow night at 7:30 p.m., and I'll handle the rest?

Unknown: Text me your address, and I'll be there.

I'd be here too. I'd also be scared to death.

Handsome, charming, funny, and a freaking football god?

Yeah, Leo was dream man material, and I, Gemma Holden, was about to have my chance at the dream.

Chapter Fourteen

Leo

Freshly showered and fully dressed, I locked my front door and headed for my Durango. But just before I hopped inside, my phone vibrated in my pocket.

I bobbled it in my hand as I slid into the driver's seat and hit accept with my index finger by the third ring.

"You shut down the Reddit thread?" Cam said by way of greeting into my ear.

"What?" I questioned, pushing the key into the ignition and clicking the engine to life.

"You shut down the Reddit thread," he repeated, and I squinted my brow in confusion.

"How'd you know that?" It'd been less than twenty-four hours since I'd put the kibosh on the online mystery girl search, and I'd been fairly certain I was the only one outside of internet trolls to remember it existed. Fuck, we'd been seven sheets to the wind when we created it.

"Because I check that fucker daily."

"You've been following that thread?"

"Are you kidding me?" he tossed out on a laugh. "That thread was gold. My sole source of online entertainment for the past two months."

Jesus Christ. *So much for being too drunk that night to remember it.*

"What gives, man?" he questioned. "Why'd you have to take away our fun?"

"*Our* fun?"

He laughed again. "Sorry to break it to you, sweetheart, but half the damn team has been following that thread. Hell, even Wes Lancaster got a few good chuckles from it. After giving us a stern lecture about the guidelines for social media, of course."

"Wow," I muttered. "Talk about music to my ears."

"Hey, if it makes you feel any better, when you get past all the laughs at your expense, we were all just rooting for you to find your girl."

"Oh yeah," I muttered sarcastically. "That's real fucking touching, Cam. Hold on a minute while I wipe away the sentimental tears."

His hearty chuckle filled my ear. "So, I guess you've officially given up your search, huh?"

"Well..." I paused, unsure if I wanted to reveal the truth of my situation, but he jumped on my hesitation with lightning-quick speed.

"Well, what?"

"Well...I shut down the thread because I found her."

"No shit?"

"No shit."

"I knew that thread was fucking genius!" he exclaimed. "You're welcome, by the way."

"Slow your celebratory roll, dude," I said through a soft chuckle. "It wasn't because of the thread."

"Explain yourself, son."

"Nonna is actually the one who found her."

His confusion was evident. "What the fuck is a Nonna?"

"She's my great-aunt."

Silence consumed the line for a few beats before Cam's voice filled my ear again.

"Let me get this straight," he started. "Your great-aunt found the mystery girl you peed on? How in the fuck does that happen?" he asked and then burst into a fit of laughter.

"Gemma works for her."

"Who the hell is Gemma?"

I rolled my eyes. "Gemma is her name."

"Whose name? Your Nonnie's name?"

"Jesus Christ, keep up, man," I muttered. "Gemma is *her* name. The mystery girl. And it's *Nonna*, not Nonnie."

"Damn, son, you really know how to make shit complicated," he responded. "Shit, I can't wait to deliver this news to Sean. He's going to have a fucking field day with this."

"Glad I could provide the entertainment for the evening."

"Man, you have no idea," Cam said on a soft laugh. "And, speaking of evening," he added. "That's actually why I was calling you. We're grabbing a few beers at Maloney's. You game?"

I couldn't deny it was nice to feel accepted by my teammates as more than just the rookie they liked to screw with, but my sights were set on bigger and better things than yucking it up with the guys.

Tonight was the night I'd been waiting what felt like ages for.

It was date night. With *my* mystery girl. With *Gemma*.

"I appreciate that, man, but I've already got plans."

"Painting your toenails and writing poetry doesn't count."

"That's tomorrow night," I corrected with a laugh. "Tonight, I'm taking Gemma out."

"Well, shit," he said, and a low wolf whistle filled my ears. "You don't waste any time."

"Nope." I grinned. "At least, not when it comes to her."

"Damn, what's with this girl?" he asked.

"I don't know, man," I muttered. Because honestly, I really didn't know what exactly drew me toward her. I just knew I wanted to get closer to her. I wanted to *know* her. Not to mention, the one million fantasies I'd conjured in my mind that had her playing the starring role. "She's just… There's just something there."

Cam's momentary pause was just enough time for me to end the conversation before he had a chance to toss out more sarcastic commentary.

"Speaking of which," I said into the receiver. "I gotta run. Talk later, dude."

A mere fifteen seconds later, I was off the phone and pulling out onto the main road.

The drive to Gemma's apartment in Brooklyn was a long one, both literally and figuratively.

Since getting drafted by the Mavericks and finding an apartment close to the stadium, I'd learned a thing or two about living outside of the city.

Number one: Getting there from anywhere else, no matter how close it seemed, took a while.

And number two: Almost no one lived in actual Manhattan.

Hoboken. Weehawken. Brooklyn. The suburbs in New Jersey. I'd been to the houses and apartments of many a player all over the tri-state area at this point, and even if lost without the help of GPS, I was pretty sure I could find my way.

But keeping my gas tank close to full was imperative, and I never went anywhere with an expectation that it would take me under thirty minutes.

Unfortunately, no matter the planning, I was running ten minutes late, and texting on the streets of Brooklyn was like asking for death.

I just hoped when I arrived, Gemma would be waiting and something less than passive-aggressively angry.

Pulling the Durango into an empty spot, I shut off the engine and hopped out as quickly as I could, jogging down the block to the address Gemma had texted me the day before.

I bounded up the steps toward the door, ready to rap my knuckles against it, but it swung open without prompt.

Gemma looked up from the ground with a sweeping lift of her head and stepped out onto the stoop, and I had to reach up to grip my chest as she did.

Heels, skinny jeans, and a delightfully low-cut blouse paid tribute to her body, and her hair fell down around her perfect face in soft waves.

I smiled big and wide and unbidden, and her forward motion pulled up short.

"You…look amazing," I breathed without thought.

She blushed, a fine rosiness I was starting to become well-acquainted with, and smiled. "Thank you."

"You're welcome," I said with ease and held out a hand for her own.

She hesitated slightly but completed the connection much more quickly than she had at lunch the day prior, and I helped her down the stairs in her heels.

"I'm sorry I'm a little late," I remarked.

"That's okay," she dismissed easily. "I know how Brooklyn can be sometimes."

Instantly, relief lightened the pressure inside my chest.

Thank God she's not mad.

I nodded my gratitude with a smile and walked her down the block to my car.

She climbed in as I opened the door without comment, and once she was securely in the passenger seat, I shut the door and rounded the hood toward the driver's side.

I knew if I was going to get through this night, I needed to figure out how to untie my tongue, but there was just something about her that robbed me of my normal self-assuredness.

She was sweet and interesting—and fucking prettier than anyone I'd ever seen.

Believe it or not, I didn't want to fuck it up.

"I tried to plan enough time, but apparently, I'm not that good at planning," I said teasingly as I climbed inside.

She smiled at my awkward excuse, and internally, I grimaced.

Good Lord, get it together, Leo.

"So, where am I headed?"

"I'm really not sure of the name of it," she said with a self-conscious laugh. "My friend suggested it, but I've got an address."

"Works for me," I said with a smile before handing her my phone. "Go ahead and punch it in, and we'll just GPS it."

Her eyes went wide, and I paused.

"What?"

She laughed a little and shook her head. "Sorry. I just…I guess it just surprised me that you handed me your phone so easily."

I chuckled and clicked on the engine with a flick of my wrist. "Don't worry. I cleared all of the incriminating stuff off of there before I left home."

"Ah," she said through a cute little giggle. "Naked pictures?"

"Tons," I confirmed teasingly. "Loads of numbers too. Maybe even a text or two from women tonight."

She narrowed her eyes, and I laughed outright. "I'm kidding. I'm a little too busy to have women all over the place."

"I'm sure that's what all the pro football players say."

With one last laugh, I shifted into drive and pulled out as she set the navigation to play, and a comfortable silence settled over us.

Both of us were nervous, I could tell, but the little bout of banter had at least eased the tension.

When we pulled up to the address listed in the phone, all the anxiousness had left her smile.

At least…until she saw the sign on the building.

"What the hell?" she yelled, and I looked up to follow her gaze.

Bright pink and neon, the letters of the sign glittered and glistened the name of the restaurant. *Drag.*

Not to mention, a seven-foot-tall Barbra Streisand standing beneath the hot-pink awning of the establishment put out her cigarette on the brick of the building and went back inside. Instantly, Gemma sank into her seat and covered her eyes.

ributionribution going to kill Abby."

Somehow, the level of her frustration just made me feel at ease.

Hell, it even made me grin a little. I'd thought she was cute when she was bumbling and awkward, but fuck, that cuteness multiplied by ten when frustration took over her pretty little face and furrowed her brow.

My chest expanded with excitement, and I exited the vehicle and rounded the hood to get to Gemma's door.

I opened it with ease and then asked the question of the night.

"Shall we?" I asked with a little smirk.

She uncovered her face, and despite the uncertainty that still remained within her pretty blue eyes, she accepted with a quiet "Yes."

It seemed we shall.

Chapter Fifteen

Gemma

I took a sip from my vodka martini and tried to wrap my brain around the chaos.

Not only was I out with a guy I'd met under the most incredibly awkward circumstances, but I'd also inadvertently brought us to a drag show for our first date.

And, Lord Almighty, Leo Landry was a sight inside the glittered-up establishment.

He stuck out like a dick in a pair of panty hose, and that was saying a lot considering our current location.

Confused and slightly concerned, I snuck my phone out of my purse and sent Abby a text message.

Me: So…uh…just out of curiosity…have you ever been to this restaurant?

She responded a minute later.

Abby: Oh yeah, I go there all the time.

Internally, I sighed at her words.

Fucking hell, I should've known…

Me: So you're 100% aware you sent me to a drag show? For a first date? With a guy I've already incurred one too many awkward encounters with?

Abby: Completely aware, and in my personal opinion, it's the most brilliant thing I've ever suggested. First dates shouldn't be stuffy and boring. They should be fun, Gem. And trust me, you're going to have some fucking fun tonight.

Either she was an evil genius, or she'd just set me up for disaster.

I honestly didn't know, but I knew spending my night distracted and texting with my best friend wasn't going to help the situation.

But before I slipped my phone back into my purse, she sent one final message.

Abby: Have fun! And, btw, if you see Asia, tell her Abby says hello.

I rolled my eyes. Oh yeah, I'd be sure to tell Asia that Abby said hello, you know, once I figured out how in the hell I was going to explain to Leo how I managed to drag—*pun intended*—us into this situation.

He took a sip of beer and his Adam's apple bobbed when the liquid went down his throat. I'd never really thought an Adam's apple could be sexy, but somehow, Leo proved otherwise.

Between his blue as the Caribbean eyes and his perfect lips and his incredibly toned and fit body, I was damn near overstimulated. It was like stepping inside a bakery on a Sunday morning and trying to pick out a goddamn pastry.

Cinnamon roll or glazed twist or strawberry-filled or…? Son of a sugar rush, just give me one of everything.

Obviously, Leo looked a lot different from a glazed donut, but I had a feeling he probably tasted just as flipping good.

When I caught myself with my mouth hanging open wide enough to catch flies, I curbed my randy thoughts and focused on taking a sip from my martini. The liquid stung as it slid down my throat, but the distraction was much-needed.

"So…uh… Interesting date choice," Leo said, and a smile perked up the corners of his lips.

"Do you want to leave?" I asked and grimaced slightly. "I seriously won't be offended if you want to go."

"Hell no." He shook his head. "But I do have a quick question before they start the show."

"Yeah?"

He leaned closer and whispered into my ear, "Are you supposed to tip the performers?" he asked. "Like at a strip club?"

"I *think* you're supposed to," I said, and then couldn't stop myself from tossing in my own question. "So…you go to strip clubs often, Leo?" I asked with a teasing smile.

"I plead the fifth, sweetheart." He simply chuckled and stood. "And, on that note, I'll be right back."

I nodded. "I'll be here." *You know, sitting inside this booth wondering why I ever trust Abby with anything and silently praying that nothing super weird happens.*

A few minutes later, Leo made his way back to our cozy booth, and once he slid in beside me, he placed a large stack of one-dollar bills in my hand.

"What's this for?" I glanced between him and the money. "I mean, I know I'm amazing company, but…?"

"Tips," he said with a little smirk. "If we're going to have our first date at a drag show, you can bet your cute ass we're going to do it right."

The next question blurted from my lips before I could stop it. "You think I have a cute ass?"

He winked and I blushed.

Hot damn, Leo Landry thought I had a cute ass.

I probably shouldn't have been so giddy over that tidbit of information, but no lie, it made me nearly euphoric. Hell, I almost asked him to rate my supposed cute ass on a scale of zero to ten, but the stage started to liven up and grabbed both Leo's and my attention before I could take that line of conversation any further.

The lights in the restaurant dimmed, and colorful reds and oranges and pinks started to highlight the stage from not one but four disco balls hanging from the ceiling, while a spotlight lit up an extremely tall and beautiful drag queen standing center stage.

"Welcome to Drag!" she exclaimed as she glided across the stage in the tallest pair of shoes I'd ever seen in my life. "Who is ready to get this show started?" she asked, and her bright red lips curled up into a smile. She fluttered her long lashes and sashayed her narrow hips around the stage as the pounding beats of "Supermodel" started to liven up the joint.

"I'm Asia," she introduced herself with a sexy little smirk. "And I'll be your main queen tonight!"

And then, one by one, Asia announced the performers for the evening as they filed onto the stage.

"Miss Fortune!"

"Halle Berries!"

"Queen Bee!"

"Mariah Kiss!"

"Duchess!"

"Betty Spears!"

The gang was all here and strutting across the stage fiercer than the Naomi Campbells and Cindy Crawfords of the world.

I couldn't deny I was fucking mesmerized.

"You better work, girls!" Asia exclaimed, her big, blond wig shifting across her shoulders and her fingers snapping three times through the air.

The crowd hooted and hollered, and it didn't take long before I joined in. I clapped my hands and cheered the queens on, and to my utter surprise, Leo was right there with me. With a giant grin etched across his mouth, he put two fingers to his lips and whistled toward the stage.

Weirdly enough, a girlish giggle escaped my throat, and I swooned a little at the sight of him—smiling and cheering on these gorgeous queens like he was a goddamn regular.

Leo Landry was so freaking comfortable in his own skin and so open-minded, not only did he take it all in stride, but he also made a point to enjoy himself.

I'd thought he was handsome the first time I'd laid eyes on him. But I was finding the more layers of himself he revealed, the more attractive he became.

It was safe to say I was *really* starting to dig Leo Landry.

And I couldn't deny that maybe, *just maybe*, the whole drag show first date idea wasn't so ridiculous after all…

Nearly an hour and a half later, dinner had been served and con-sumed, another round of drinks achieved, and we were nearing the final act of the night.

Duchess stood on the stage, her wig a black homage to Cher and her outfit inspired by a Las Vegas showgirl. "Fellow queens and drinkers of booze!" she exclaimed into the mic. "It has been brought to my attention that we have a very, *very* special guest here tonight."

The crowd excitedly hummed their response, and I lifted my sec-ond martini to my lips for a sip as I glanced around the room for some kind of secret celebrity hiding out in the back booths.

If Bradley Cooper is here tonight, I will drop dead right here be-tween the queens.

"Do you want to know who it is?" Duchess asked, and her pink-painted lips crested up into a huge smile as she moved her gaze around the crowd.

When a guy from the back shouted "Tell us!" she rolled her eyes dramatically.

"Oh, honey, you're far too excitable," she purred. "My sympathies go out to anyone who fucks you."

The crowd laughed.

"Okay, okay...I won't keep you in suspense any longer," Duchess finally continued. "Our special guest of the night is handsome as fuck and a strapping young football star to boot. Not to mention, I have no doubt he will help our favorite New York Mavericks finally bring home the championship this year!"

My eyes went wide, and I nearly choked on my martini.

Oh no...

Unless there were other Mavericks hiding out in Drag, it was safe to say Leo had officially been spotted.

Oh God...

My breath got caught in my lungs as I braced myself in anticipation.

"Tonight," Duchess exclaimed, "Leo Landry is in the house!" The spotlight moved from the stage and directly onto our booth. And before I knew it, both Leo and I were squinting against the harsh glare.

"Come on up here, honey!" Duchess purred. "It's not every day we get a man like you inside our little establishment!"

I looked at Leo, and he looked at me.

"I think I've been outed," he whispered through a chuckle, and a relieved giggle escaped my lips.

"It appears that way," I whispered back. "And sorry to break this to you, but I don't think we're going to be able to leave unless you get onstage."

"Fucking hell." He chuckled again.

It didn't take long before everyone inside Drag started chanting his name and, eventually, with a slightly embarrassed grin stretched across his lips, Leo stood up and headed toward the front of the room.

The instant he stepped onto the stage beside Duchess, the whole damn crowd started hooting and hollering crazy shit toward him.

"Flex your muscles!"

"Dance with Duchess!"

And my personal favorite, "Take off your pants!"

Well, mostly because it came from my slightly boozed-up lips, but same difference, right?

"It appears you're quite the hot commodity," Duchess purred into the mic, and Leo ran a hand through his hair on a laugh. "What brings you here tonight, sugar?"

He pointed one index finger toward me. "That pretty lady right there."

Duchess squinted her eyes as she took in my appearance and then tsked under her breath. "And here I thought I might be the one who gets to take you home tonight. Now I'm not so sure I can compete with Ms. Down Home Bombshell over there."

He could only laugh in response.

The queen sighed dramatically at the crowd before bringing her gaze back to Leo. "Is she your girlfriend?"

"No." He shook his head and then grinned wickedly. "Well, at least, *not yet*."

Not yet?

My heart started pounding inside my chest at his words.

Not yet, as in he saw it as an actual possibility?

Not yet, as in he wanted me to be his girlfriend?

I was equal parts excited and scared.

Let's not get too carried away here, Gem, I mentally coached myself. *The man is onstage with a drag queen dressed up as Cher, for fuck's sake. Just take a breath and don't read too much into shit.*

"Not yet?" Duchess tilted her head to the side and searched Leo's gaze. "What the fuck does that mean?"

"This is our first date."

"And she brought your ass to a drag show?"

He smirked. "Yeah."

"Good for you, honey!" Duchess called toward me. "But you're going to have to shut your eyes for a bit, because the other queens and I have some business with your man here. You don't mind if we play with him for a bit, do ya, sugar?"

Leo's eyes went wide and locked with mine, but I simply shook my head on a laugh.

"He's all yours!"

Duchess grinned like the cat who ate the canary, while Leo shot a playful glare in my direction. But he didn't have much time to plan an escape route because three queens strutted onto the stage and pushed his fine ass into the lone chair sitting in the center.

"Just sit back and relax, sugar," Duchess purred into the mic while the opening beats of "Whatta Man" started to play through the speakers. "We're going to take real good care of you."

Leo's eyes went even wider as the drag queens started to shower him with all sorts of attention, and by the time they were a good minute into the song, I had to put a hand over my mouth to stifle my giggles.

"Hold up! Hold up!" Asia shouted over the music as she made a slicing hand across her throat. "Stop the music for a second!" she exclaimed. "This isn't working. We need some backup to really bring this performance on home."

Duchess put a hand to her hip. "Backup?"

"Oh yes, sister." Asia winked. "And I know just the person." Before I could comprehend what was happening, she pointed her red-painted fingernail out into the crowd and what felt like directly at me.

Surely, I'm just seeing shit, right?

I looked around the room and then back at the stage.

"Get up here, honey!" Asia exclaimed, and my eyes went wide. "That's right, sista," she added with an amused smile. "We're talking about you."

Wait…*whaaaaat?*

"Seriously?" I mouthed with a hand to my chest, and she nodded.

"Get your cute ass up here and sing the hook!"

Well, *fuck.*

With the crowd now hooting and hollering for me to join Leo onstage and two queens taunting me to get off my ass, I did the only thing I could do in that situation.

I downed what was left of my martini and said fuck it. When queens demanded you get onstage and sing, you fucking got onstage and you sang.

So, that was exactly what I did.

I swallowed my nerves and walked through the crowd and toward the front of the room.

Leo grinned up at me as I took a mic from a stagehand and stepped onstage.

"Okay, honey, just to make sure we're on the same page, we're going to have to hear a few notes from you," Asia said once I stood beside her and Duchess. "We gotta make this good, and trust me, sugar, no one wants to hear some cat-screeching bullshit, okay?"

I giggled and blushed a little. "Okay…uh… What do you want me to sing?"

Both queens smiled deviously. "Sing the hook for us."

I had a feeling they were calling my bluff, that I was most likely called up onstage to be some sort of comic relief, but I simply shrugged it off and cleared my throat in preparation.

Once the DJ started playing "Whatta Man" again, I put my best En Vogue foot forward and sang the opening chorus, or the *hook,* as Asia called it.

I'd barely gotten through the first few lines before the DJ shut off the music at Asia's request.

"Oh, *honey!*" Duchess exclaimed and snapped her fingers in the air. "You done did it, girl!"

"This bitch can sing, queens!" Asia shouted toward the crowd. "She can really fucking sing!"

And Leo, well, he looked up at me from his spot in the chair with the biggest smile I'd ever seen in my life.

The damn thing went straight to my fucking brain.

High off his smile and high off doing what I loved most, I stood on that stage for the next five or so minutes with a bunch of beautiful drag queens and sang my lungs out while they grinded and danced all over Leo.

And hell if it wasn't a damn good time.

Touché, Abby. Tou-fucking-ché.

Chapter Sixteen

Leo

Streetlights and the beams of passing vehicles filled my vision as I drove back toward Gemma's apartment, and fuck, I couldn't wipe the smile from my face if I tried.

Her voice danced in my ears as she chattered on about Asia and Duchess and the thrill of the stage.

I could hear the melodic quality of it so much more easily now, and the lull of it during a bout of excitement was particularly enticing.

She'd beyond killed it up there, damn near brought the crowd *and* the queens of Drag to their fucking knees, and I was like a proud boyfriend already.

From zero to one hundred in less than a second, this adorable fucking creature had not only stolen my attention, but with sniper-like precision appeared to be going straight for my heart as well.

"I can't believe she took off her wig at the end and put it on my head." Gemma smiled at me, and my chest expanded. "I mean, I thought the hair, the makeup, all of that stuff was like sacred or something."

"It is. But you were a queen up there, and her wig was the best she could do in the way of a crown," I said with a laugh.

She giggled and playfully shoved my shoulder, and it was safe to say we were miles away from the awkward, quiet mess we'd been on the way to Drag a few hours ago.

Apparently, her friend Abby who'd recommended the spot knew a thing or two about loosening Gemma up.

And fuck, it had worked like a charm.

Right before my very eyes, I'd had the pleasure of watching Gemma blossom and bloom into a comfortable ease. She'd let down her guard, and I'd been entranced by each facet of her delightful, quirky personality that she'd revealed to me.

To say she was something special was putting it mildly.

This girl, my mystery girl, was unlike anyone I'd ever met.

"So, I have to ask," I said and smirked at her out of my periphery. "Where in the hell have you been hiding that voice?"

She blushed at the compliment but quickly transferred any embarrassment to cute and sassy attitude.

"What? Like I've had so many opportunities to show it off for you?" She laughed. "This is our first date, in case you've forgotten, and our encounters before this included spilled pee and your aunt Alma."

"I'm surprised Alma hasn't built a stage in her house for you. She's a real pusher."

She scoffed. "I'm not *that* good. And she doesn't know. It's not like I spend my days singing for her."

"Well, you should," I said, and she rolled her eyes. "Hell, you should be singing for anyone within a one-thousand-mile radius, Gem. Your gorgeous fucking voice should be serenading me through the goddamn radio," I added seriously, but she just brushed it off.

"Don't be ridiculous." Her soft laugh was dubious. "I mean, I know I don't know what I'm supposed to be doing, but I'm pretty damn certain I'm not star material."

I completely disagreed. She had the voice and she had the look in spades, but I didn't see much point in arguing about it with her.

Instead, I asked another question piqued by her uncertainty.

"Why don't you know what you're supposed to be doing? You mean, career-wise?"

"Yep." She nodded. "I don't have a fucking clue."

"You're not interested in doing anything specific?"

She shook her head. "I was in school…well, I was almost done with school." She chuckled self-consciously. "I almost had my degree. The one in engineering my whole family expected me to get."

"Engineering wasn't for you?"

"Uh…*no.* I realized I wasn't happy. Like, at all. And as I pictured myself getting closer and closer to graduation—and the job I'd be expected to get—it all started to seem terrible. I mean…doing something I hate for the rest of my life? No thanks."

"I can understand that," I said, and I could. "Your family doesn't?"

She shrugged. "It's not what they planned."

I nodded silently, wondering what it would have been like if my family hadn't been supportive of my career.

Hell, they definitely could have snubbed it. It wasn't like the dream of playing professional football was one without risk. Most people with that goal never made it.

As if she read my mind, she turned the conversation on me.

"What about you? Have you always wanted to play football?"

"Definitely." I nodded and smiled. "I've been into it since I was a kid. Bonus was that I turned out to be pretty good at it. Passion is great, but I wouldn't have gotten anywhere without a little luck."

"Yeah, but I'm sure you worked hard."

"Every day. Conditioning, training. I made sure I had the best shot possible."

She sighed. "I wish I had that kind of drive."

"I'm sure you do," I said easily. "Maybe you just haven't found the right thing yet."

"I guess not," she said and picked at an invisible piece of lint from her blouse. "That's why I took the temp job. I figured something would spark my interest at some point."

"So being a medical tech wasn't your dream job?"

"Not quite." Her laughter was music to my ears.

"Thank God. I'd feel really bad about costing you it if it had been."

"That wasn't your fault. I dropped it."

"I bobbled the handoff," I said easily, and she just giggled.

"Trust me, Leo, that whole fiasco was *my* fault, not yours."

Pulling up in front of her apartment, I shut off the engine, hopped out of the car, and rounded the hood before helping Gemma out of the passenger side.

Quietly, we walked hand in hand toward her apartment building, and when we stopped just beneath the awning covering the front entrance, her gaze locked with mine, and once again, her face bloomed into a breathtaking blush.

Fuck, I loved that blush of hers.

"I've gotta be honest, Gemma…" I paused, and her throat bobbed a bit as she swallowed nervously.

"Yeah?"

"Tonight was probably the best date I've ever had."

"Really?"

"Really," I confirmed, easing forward slightly to prepare to make my move. "There's just one thing that will ensure it holds that title forever."

"What?" she asked softly.

"This."

Smooth but swift, I leaned toward her, sank a hand into her beautiful hair, and sealed my lips to hers. She gasped in surprise, and I took the opportunity to slide my tongue inside.

Sweet melons and martinis, she tasted the best of anything I'd ever consumed in my entire life, and I dove deeper. I took more of her mouth as her body melted into the kiss, and I twisted some of her hair around my fingers.

God, she felt good. Tasted good. Everything that revolved around Gemma was good, even when it came to how she made me feel.

And I wanted more. Fuck, did I want more.

But for some insane reason, I didn't want to rush this. I didn't want to screw anything up when it came to her. I wanted to take my time, even if it meant leaving her apartment with a throbbing case of blue balls.

We danced and pushed with our tongues a bit longer, and just before I crossed the point of no return, I placed one final kiss to her perfect lips and pulled away.

I watched the way her pretty little lashes moved downward with each blink, and when her blue gaze locked with mine again, the responding smile that teased across her lips had my head spinning from the beauty and buzz of it all.

I didn't want to leave her, but I didn't want to do something rash because my dick demanded instant gratification.

"I'll call you," I said simply. Complex words weren't possible.

She nodded, and I smiled at the thought that maybe, for her, words weren't possible at all.

"Goodnight, Gemma."

"Goodnight, Leo."

I'll see you soon.

Chapter Seventeen

Gemma

I was high as a kite once I stepped inside my apartment.

With the door a silent click behind me, I rested my back against the wall, and the girliest little sigh left my lungs.

Leo kissed me.

He. *Kissed.* Me.

And, holy leprechauns, it was a "Lucky Charms in kiss form" kind of magically delicious kiss.

That kiss started out with a gentle press of Leo's lips to mine, but it hadn't ended there.

No way, Jose. That sucker traveled straight into my chest, down to my belly, and landed in my fucking toes.

I felt like Meg Ryan and Julia Roberts and Reese Witherspoon and Kate Winslet all wrapped up into one real-life, swoony as fuck, this feels like a fucking movie kind of moment.

That kiss made my eyes cross and my foot pop up as if it'd been yanked by a marionette's string.

I was still dizzy just thinking about it.

What a glorious fucking night.

I sighed into the silence of my apartment, and to my surprise,

Abby didn't pop up from the couch to scare the ever-living crap out of me.

"Abby?" I called out, but even after a few seconds, got nothing in return.

It seemed as though my pseudo-roommate was MIA for the evening.

For the first time in a long time, I was kind of disappointed by that reality.

I needed to gab and recount the night's events. I needed to tell someone about my drag show singing escapades. I needed to make puppy eyes over the memories of Leo. And I needed to turn into a real-life heart eyes emoji as I told someone, *any-fucking-one,* about that kiss.

But it seemed the only company I had for the rest of the night was me, myself, and I.

Accepting my silent fate, I pushed myself off the wall and headed into the bathroom to get ready for bed.

Surely, I could fill the duration of my evening with funny pet videos on Instagram before sleep took over.

I did the normal nightly routine—wash my face, brush my teeth, and pee—and by the time I crawled into my bed, my face was clear of makeup, my hair was tossed up into a messy bun, and my coziest pajamas cradled my body.

I had no idea how I would get any sleep with the way my brain was so damn fixated on everything that was Leo, but I was really hoping cute videos of furbabies would be enough to take my mind off of him so sleep would be an option.

Under the covers and well into my fourth video—*this one, a sleepy golden retriever puppy dressed in duck pajamas*—I couldn't stop myself from replaying the evening in my head.

The drag show.

Leo's smile.

Dinner.

Leo's eyes.

Singing onstage.

Leo's kiss.

And by the time I'd replayed the whole date a good five or six times in my head, I started to worry that maybe I was jumping the gun a bit. I mean, this wasn't Joe Schmo working at the deli up the street I was thinking about here.

It was *Leo Fucking Landry*, a professional football god for the New York Mavericks.

He was insanely handsome, incredibly successful, and no doubt had millions of other girls vying for his attention.

And me? Well, I was a clumsy and quirky girl who had no real career prospects in sight.

I had no degree.

I quit college during my senior year.

And I was currently the girl who packed up his great-aunt's sex toys.

Did those things equate to a match made in heaven? I wasn't exactly convinced.

But I refused to be so flipping negative.

Leo said he'd call me. And, well, if he was truly interested, he'd call.

Other than that, it was out of my control.

Just focus on that alpaca with the hat on and stop worrying over it, Gem, I coached myself.

Luckily, it worked.

Another few videos in and after a quick status check on Ariana Grande's recent Instagram posts, my blinks turned longer and eventually my eyes started to fall closed.

Ah, yes, the glorious angel named sleep. I sure do love when she visits.

I was just on the brink of being lights-out, but my heart damn near jumped out of my throat when my phone started ringing and vibrating in my lap.

My eyes popped open, and I squinted as I tried to look at the far too bright screen.

Incoming Call: Leo.

I blinked three times just to make sure it was really him.

Spoiler alert: It was.

He'd dropped me off at my apartment not even two hours ago, and he was already calling me?

Maybe it's an accidental butt dial? I thought to myself, just before I answered on the fourth ring.

"Hello?" I said into the receiver, fully expecting to hear complete silence or muffled sounds of rustling and movement.

But, to my utter surprise, he answered back.

"Hi." His voice might as well have been melted chocolate with how damn good it sounded.

"Hi," I repeated dumbly, and then cleared my throat to add, "Uh…is everything okay?"

"Everything is perfect."

Everything is perfect.

I smiled like a lunatic. "Well, that's good news."

"It is," he agreed. "So, what are you doing right now?"

"Lying in my bed."

"Shit," he muttered. "Did I wake you up?"

"No," I lied, but thought better of it. "Well, sort of, but I won't hold it against you."

He chuckled at that. "Sorry I woke you."

"It's fine," I said. "So, is there a reason you're calling me, or…?"

"I'm a man of my word, Gemma. When I say I'll call, I'll call."

"And apparently, you're extremely prompt," I teased.

"What can I say?" he asked on a laugh. "I really want to see you again."

I smiled to my goddamn toes. "Yeah?"

"Yeah," he said, his voice deep and husky. "So, Gemma Holden, what do you think about another date with me?"

"I think I'd probably be interested in something like that…"

"*Probably* interested?" he questioned, and soft sarcasm rounded the edges of his voice.

"Okay, *very* interested."

"That's more like it," he said on a soft laugh. "*But* I do have one special request."

"And what's that?"

More kissing? Showing me your penis? Hot sex?

"*I* get to choose the date this time."

I was only slightly disappointed by his response, but still, Leo Landry wanted to take me out on a second date. *Yes, please!*

I pulled the receiver from my ear, pushed my face into my pillow and squealed.

Once I got my shit together, I cleared my throat and said, "Deal."

Two minutes later and it was official.

Next week, after he got back from his away game in Charlotte, we'd second date it right the fuck up.

Game on, Leonard.

Chapter Eighteen

Leo

The energy was amped and the smell of sweat was rampant as the sound of cleated feet stomped into the locker room in Charlotte stadium.

Another win and another glorious week of feeling like we had a chance at the championship this year.

I wasn't a standout player by any stretch of the imagination, but I'd done my part, and that was all I could really hope for as the weeks kept ticking.

"Good game, Leo," Cam said with a smack to my back as he walked by me on the way to his locker.

"You too," I said back, smiling at the superstar who'd somehow become my friend. I'd spent years looking up to the guy, watching his games on TV, and trying to learn something from him, and as fate would have it, it seemed he was turning into one of my closest friends.

Life was so funny that way.

"I'm impressed by your coverage," he added. "And I know the other guys are too. Sean already said he wants to run some drills with you this week. Get a little one-on-one action to give you some experience with the best receiver in the league." He rolled his eyes at Sean's obvious ego, and I just laughed.

The opportunity to work with guys like this was mind-blowing, no matter how cocky they were.

"Great. Tell him to expect a run for his money."

Cam laughed at my arrogance and winked. "Oh, don't worry. I can't wait to tell him that."

He jumped up from the bench and slapped me on the shoulder.

"He's gonna run your ass off for it, though."

I grinned. "Good."

Cam nodded his approval, and everything inside me sighed. I couldn't believe how easily I'd taken to the team and the guys, and how right my career choice felt. It honestly felt like I was exactly where I should be, doing what I was meant to do.

Of course, that kind of security only made me think of Gemma and how she didn't know.

I just didn't understand how she couldn't. The instant she'd opened her mouth and starting singing along with the queens on-stage, it'd been clear to me *and* everyone else inside Drag what she should be doing and then some.

She was talented. So fucking talented.

And beyond that, you could tell she lived for it. Breathed for it.

Like she was meant to be onstage.

I just wasn't sure how to get her to see it.

Opening my locker, I grabbed my bag from the hook and set it on the bench in front of me to get some clothes and a towel for my shower. But before I could pull out my T-shirt, the bottom of the bag buzzed against the wood of the bench, the loud sound echoing against the metal of the lockers.

I fished around in the bottom until my fingers closed around my phone and I pulled it out.

Several texts from Gemma lit up the screen, and I immediately clicked to open them, shower plans long forgotten.

Gemma: Your aunt is right. You do have the cutest butt on the field.

Gemma: Wow. You're fast. Like, cheetah speed. Remind me not to be chased by you. I'd be lunch meat just like a gazelle.

Gemma: That guy was HUGE. Did he injure you?

Gemma: Oh wait, I guess you can't really answer right now, huh? Fuck, I hope he didn't injure you.

Gemma: Oh, never mind, I just watched you tackle some guy to the ground. You're good to go, if you're wondering.

Gemma: Wow. These games are long. Aren't you tired? I'm kind of tired.

Gemma: How many minutes do you have to run a day not to die doing this?

Gemma: Holy shit, that guy is missing teeth. Is there a chance you're going to be missing teeth at any point? Tell me now.

I laughed at her running commentary, noting how good she was at a one-sided conversation. Apparently, she'd been hanging around my aunt Alma a little too long.

Me: If I get teeth knocked out, I'll go to a dentist. Don't worry. I'm not sure I could pull off the hockey player look.

I waited with the phone in my hand for her answer, but when it didn't come quickly, I knew I couldn't sit around waiting forever.

I had to get my ass showered and ready for the bus back to the hotel if I didn't want to be on the team's shitlist.

Tossing my phone back into my bag, I ran to the showers and did just that.

I scrubbed and soaped and washed everywhere, but what I absolutely didn't do was think of Gemma. The last thing I needed in a group shower with a bunch of football players was a boner I couldn't hide.

Dried off and dressed, I grabbed my bag and headed for the bus.

My phone was still silent, and disappointment niggled deep in my gut.

Cam smiled as I climbed aboard and nodded to the empty seat beside him.

I took it without question.

"Get pretty enough in there? Tampon secure and everything?" he asked just as my ass hit the seat.

Apparently, my version of quick hadn't been quick enough.

"I didn't have time for makeup, but I made do," I said through a laugh and slid my bag to the ground at my feet and settled my head into the rest.

"You better buck up," he said as I closed my eyes. "We've got celebrating to do."

I was shaking my head before he even finished the sentence. "I don't think so, man. I'm gonna stay in tonight."

"Wow. Period cramps must be really bad."

I rolled my eyes and laughed. "First day *is* always the heaviest."

He smirked at that. "Fine, fine. I guess I'll let you off the hook. *This* time. But that's mostly because it doesn't take a fucking genius to figure out why."

I quirked a brow, and he chuckled.

"Mystery girl who isn't such a mystery anymore," he added, and I couldn't exactly deny it. "How was the big date, by the way?"

"So good we've already got plans to go out tomorrow night when I get back."

"Damn, son," Cam said and feigned wiping tears from his eyes, "It appears our little rook is about to turn into a man right before our very eyes."

I just laughed it off, and he grinned.

"Anyway, I already knew your ass wasn't going out tonight the minute we left the field."

"Then why'd you give me so much shit?" I asked with a grin.

He shrugged. "For fun."

"And what exactly are you doing tonight?"

"Going to the room and calling Lana," he said with a wink and a nudge, and a mere ten seconds later he put his headphones on and turned to look out the window.

That was the Cam Mitchell version of *conversation officially dismissed.*

And, as much as my phone burned at my feet, I knew better than to take it out on the bus. Instead, I closed my eyes and settled in for the ride back to the hotel.

When I got there, I'd call Gemma.

Maybe even FaceTime her.

Chapter Nineteen

Gemma

Sunday nights were for Netflix binges and takeout.

Also, when you worked at Alma's sex toy sweatshop, they were for calling it an early night and getting some sleep in preparation for the week ahead.

At a little after ten, I climbed into bed, set my alarm for 7:00 a.m., and bid the lights good night. I needed at least eight solid hours of sleep if I wanted any chance of keeping up with ole Alma and her plethora of shipments.

Not to mention, she'd recently put me in charge of taking inventory photos. An entire overhaul of product pictures, to be exact. Once I'd managed to convince her the weirdness that was vibrators in nature landscapes wasn't easy on the eyes, she'd given me free rein on revamping the whole vibe—pun intended—of Alma's Secrets.

And, in the spirit of keeping shit up to the sex toy industry standards, I went with the simplicity of white backgrounds and great lightning. It didn't take much to make a fake penis stand out.

You're welcome, by the way.
And for anyone who was subjected to seeing their favorite

vibrator sitting on a park bench, I'd like to apologize on behalf of Alma for your trauma.

Thankfully, I was able to push tomorrow's long list of work to-do's out of my head and shut my eyes.

Sleep had been the number one man in my life for as long as I could remember.

Well, sleep and Adam Levine.

I'd been a Maroon 5 fan *forever*. We're talking in-utero crushing. If I ever found the musical balls to audition for *The Voice*, you could bet your sweet ass I'd be Team Adam all the livelong day.

But that was a pipe dream.

I'd be more likely to run into Adam Levine at the fucking dollar spot at Target than meet him while auditioning on an internationally known reality show.

But, sleep? Well, he wasn't a mere pipe dream. He was the real deal. My main squeeze.

And he and I were about to get all kinds of up close and personal.

I shut my eyes and my breathing slowed, and just before my nocturnal Casanova wrapped his big, strong arms around me, my phone vibrated across my nightstand and echoed off the otherwise silent walls of my bedroom.

With my eyes still closed, I groaned and turned over onto my side to haphazardly grab my phone. Once the little vibrating bitch was in my hands, I peeked my eyes open to find *Incoming FaceTime Call: Leo* flashing across the screen.

FaceTime? What the hell?

For no apparent reason besides pure shock, my heart pounded inside my chest, and I hid myself *and* my phone under the covers.

Why was he FaceTiming me?

Besides the embarrassing urine collection session and the awkward lunch with his great-aunt, we'd been on one date.

Surely, that did not translate to FaceTime calls.

Text messages? Of course.

Phone calls? Definitely.

But FaceTime? I don't think so, Leonard.

We hadn't reached the date number five threshold where I started showing myself sans makeup and living my truth of being a real girl who poops and has a tendency to get all kinds of bitchy on days one through three of her period.

As of right now, with only date number one in the history books?

I was a glowing, airbrushed goddess who never had to shit, smelled of roses after a five-mile run, and only ate portion-appropriate meals.

I sure as fuck didn't answer FaceTime calls in the middle of the night when I looked like Hagrid from *Harry Potter*.

I had a rep to protect until I'd *fully* won him over with my girlish charm.

Thankfully, the vibrating rings came to a halt and a missed FaceTime call tallied itself in my call log.

I stared at my phone and tried to comprehend the situation, and eventually, came to the conclusion that it had to have been an accidental FaceTime call.

A FaceTime butt dial, so to speak.

With my fingers to the keys, I tapped out a quick text message and hit send.

Me: I think you butt-dialed me.

His response came thirty seconds later.

Leo: Why didn't you answer?

Me: Because I figured it was an accident.

Leo: But it wasn't an accident.

Shock registered itself on my face in the form of wide eyes and a parted mouth. I was the real-live version of one of the sex dolls men could purchase from Alma's site for the bargain price of $29.95.

Me: You FaceTimed me on purpose???

Leo: And that's a bad thing because…?

Me: No, not bad. Just…kind of weird.

Leo: Weird? LOL. How is that weird?

Me: Because we haven't reached date number five yet.

Leo: And date number five is when FaceTime calls are allowed? Is there some dating rule book I'm not aware of?

Me: More of a silent, unwritten rule book. It's the personal-intimacy-dam-breaching date.

Leo: I've never really been the kind of guy who plays by the rules, sweetheart. And I'm not sure how FaceTime prematurely breaches any personal intimacy barriers. Are you naked? Is that why this is a problem?

Panicked, I answered the only part of his text that seemed relevant. I wasn't just lounging around at my nudist colony retreat. As a matter of fact, I wasn't sure I'd ever wandered around my apartment naked when there wasn't a sexual reason.

Me: I'm not naked!

Leo: I'm going to FaceTime you again. How about you answer this time?

Every stubborn bone in my body stood at attention as I shook my head. My vagina wasn't blowing in the wind, but I looked like hell after a tornado. No way I was answering that call.

Me: Nope.

Leo: Answer the call, Gemma.

Me: I can't. It will ruin the whole allure. I can't have you seeing me look like Hagrid before we've even gone out on our second date.

Leo: Who is Hagrid?

Had he seriously just asked me that?
The entire fucking world and their moms should've known who Hagrid was.

Me: YOU DON'T KNOW HAGRID FROM HARRY POTTER?

Leo: Are you talking about those movies with the little wizard boy?

The little wizard boy? I didn't know whether to laugh or cry.
I mean, he was skirting around some serious Harry Potter sacrilege kind of shit at the moment.

Me: Are you fucking with me right now? Harry Potter is one of the greatest literary creations of our time.

Leo: LOL. There're books too?

Me: OMG.

Leo: Answer the phone, Gemma.

This time, he didn't give me any chance for a rebuttal. My phone started vibrating in my hands again, and I immediately hid under the covers.

Shit. He's pushy.

Against my better judgment, I accepted the damn call and prayed he couldn't actually see my face through the clouded darkness of my comforter.

Instantly, his face filled the screen, and I couldn't not smile.

Good God, he was handsome. In other words, *not* the male version of me right now.

"Gemma?" he said and squinted his eyes. "Are you there?"

"I'm here."

He chuckled. "Are you in a cave?"

"I'm under my covers."

He squinted his eyes a little harder, and eventually, a mischievous little smirk eased its way across his lips. "All right, then. I won't complain about the view."

It was then that I realized even though Leo couldn't really make out my face, because of the brightness of the screen and the fact that it was pointed directly toward the lower half of my body, he could easily see everything else. And I mean, everything else.

My braless boobs in my ratty old tank top.

My bare legs.

My lacy underwear.

"I never thought I'd be an admirer of lace with pink polka dots, but yeah, I'm officially a fan."

So much for not showing him your face, you little floozy.

"Shit." I groaned and tossed the blankets off my head and sat up with my back against the headboard.

He pouted. "Aw, Gem. I was really enjoying the cave communications."

"I'm aware." I snorted. "Looks like now you're just stuck with Hagrid."

"Well, I'm no Harry Potter expert, but if this is Hagrid, fuck, he's beautiful."

I giggled and blushed at the same time. "Don't give me your pity compliments, Leonard."

"The only pity occurring right now is that I'm ten hours away from you."

"And what would you do if you were closer?"

"I'd get in my car and join my Hagrid in bed."

I laughed. "And then what would you do?"

Leo quirked a brow. "Well, I'd start by enjoying the up close and personal view," he said, and a raspy groan escaped his lips. "Yeah, I'd enjoy the fuck out of that view."

"Then what?" I asked before I could stop the words from leaving my lips.

"Oh, sweet, beautiful, sexy Gemma, how much time do we have?" he asked, and I swear to God, he licked his lips. "Because this conversation might take a while."

Fuck, I wanted to know. *Badly.* But I also didn't want the conversation to head toward phone sex. Alma would call me Virgin Mary for avoiding it, but I wasn't ready. We were new, and I was attached. Phone sex would complicate things, and when sex started to complicate things, I at least wanted a warm body to cuddle me while I freaked out.

And with the way my body was already starting to react to his words, I didn't trust myself to stop things before they got too far.

"Nope," I said. "Never mind. I don't want to know."

"You don't want to know?"

I shook my head. "No way in hell will I let our first sexual encounter be via FaceTime."

Leo chuckled softly and waggled his brows. "Are you saying we *will* have a sexual encounter in the near future?"

I rolled my eyes. But I also smiled. "Why exactly did you call me again?"

"Because I wanted to see you," he said with a grin. "And because I wanted to make sure we were still on for tomorrow night."

"Yes, we're still on."

"Pick you up at seven?"

"I'll be ready," I whispered. "Good night, Leonard."

"Sweet dreams, Gem."

Sweet dreams? *After that call?* Yeah, right. I highly doubted there was anything sweet about the dirty, Leo-infused fantasies that were already rolling through my brain.

Chapter Twenty

Leo

Gemma's voice rolled over the words of "Black Velvet" on the stage of Minard's, a karaoke club I'd found with the help of Teeny Martinez. It was in the bowels of Manhattan, and the walls seemed like they were living, they shimmered with so much filth, but tonight was one of the best times I'd ever had in my life.

Tonight was date number two, and somehow, someway, whenever I was with Gemma, I felt like I was flying.

High off her. High off us. Fucking loving any moment that included time spent with her.

And for the second time, I had the pleasure of hearing her undeniable talent firsthand.

I sat in the crowd, at our little table in the middle of the bar, and she stood onstage with a mic to her lips and her gorgeous crooning filling my ears.

She was always beautiful, even during middle of the night FaceTime calls with messy hair and sleep-rimmed eyes, but when she was onstage, she was at her most breathtaking.

If only I could get her to realize how fucking talented she truly was.

Her voice rasped with gravel and then turned smooth as silk as she sang the final words over and over again.

If you please.

Good God, did I ever.

She was a goddess and a performer and a feisty little bright spot on the stage all at once, and the crowd was going crazy for her.

Hell, I couldn't even be mad at the bastards who stared at her with heat in their eyes.

This girl, *my girl*, was a fucking magnet you couldn't take your eyes off of.

I'd sung a song of my own, but other than a tiny moment of recognition, the crowd hadn't given me even half the ovation. And, fuck, the whole damn establishment had acknowledged my rookie status on the New York Mavericks the instant we stepped inside the front doors.

The irony of it made me smile. It made me proud. It made me feel only validation and joy for Gemma.

I loved seeing her in this element. This loose. This at *ease*.

I didn't know if I'd ever be able to take her on a date where she didn't sing, such was the siren-like call of her voice and the euphoria her performance provided.

I wasn't sure what the next stop on our dating tour could be, having already done both the drag club and the karaoke bar, but I knew it sure as hell wouldn't be a silent night at the movies.

The crowd went wild as the song came to a close, and Gemma jumped down off the stage gracefully.

My smile stretched from ear to ear as I awaited her arrival at our table, a fresh drink in her spot that I'd ordered in preparation.

She mooned over the simple gesture as she sat down, and I marveled at how easy it was to impress her.

"Nonna must treat you really awful if ordering you a drink is this impressive."

She laughed. "God, I love when you call her that, Leonard."

I rolled my eyes. "That's who she is to me."

"Yes," she agreed. "And you're Leonard to her." She smirked. "She talks about you constantly."

And for once, I was the one who blushed.

"No, she doesn't."

"Oh yes, she does. She thinks you hung the moon and the stars and then some."

I laughed. "That sure isn't how she talks to me."

"Of course it isn't. Because she also thinks you're too cocky for your own good."

"Now, that sounds more like her," I said with a roll of my eyes, and she nodded. "How do you like working for her, by the way?"

"Aside from all the dildo handling?" She shrugged. "I guess it's pretty good."

I'm sorry...what? Did she just say dildo handling?

"Aside from the what?" I asked. Surely, my ears had deceived me.

"Aside from the dildo handling."

Apparently, my ears are working just fine...

Those two words latched themselves inside my brain, and once I'd comprehended them as much as was mentally possible, my sip of beer turned right around in my throat, spraying up and out before I could stop it.

Gemma held up a hand in front of her face and squealed. "Oh my God. What is it with us and fluids?"

"I'm sorry," I said, ignoring her question completely. "Did you really just say dildos?"

"Oh no!" She covered her mouth with her hand, and her eyes widened as realization set in. "Holy crap!" she muttered behind the skin of her palm. "You didn't know?"

"Please tell me dildos is a code word for anything else besides actual dildos."

Her laugh was uproarious and long, and if it weren't for how completely exhilarating I found it, the wait might have annoyed me.

When she finally got it together, her smile was unrepentant. "What exactly do you think your aunt sells?"

"T-shirts or candles or some shit," I answered, and she giggled.

"So, I hate to break this to you, but your aunt has an online sex toy and lingerie business. That's what I do for her. Organize them and ship them out."

"You have got to be shitting me."

She shook her head vigorously. "I cannot believe you didn't know."

"Of course I didn't know! I guess that's not the sort of thing you tell your great-nephew. Fucking hell, that was way, way, way too much information for my brain to handle."

"I guess I probably shouldn't tell you who does all the inventory testing then, huh?"

I almost choked again on my beer and shook my head adamantly. "For the love of God, no more details. Let me go back to thinking my Nonna sells candles and fucking T-shirts."

Fucking hell, I knew my Nonna was a goddamn wild card, but her selling sex toys online wasn't even within the realm of possibility until about two minutes ago when Gemma had spilled the terrifying beans.

Nearly five Christmases ago, Nonna had announced to the family that she was going to start her own online store and sell T-shirts as a fun hobby.

Fucking T-shirts, *not* sex toys.

Pretty sure if she had mentioned dildos that night at Christmas dinner, none of us would've been able to finish our meals. Also, we probably wouldn't have been so damn enthusiastic for her.

We'd cheered on her new venture, completely oblivious to the fact that T-shirts weren't even close to what she'd actually had in mind.

"So..." Gemma paused for a moment, and a cute little smile kissed her lips. "Shall we table this conversation for another time, then?"

"Yeah," I muttered. "How about we reschedule it for never? The less I know about my Nonna peddling dildos online, the better."

She snorted then, trying to contain her laughter and failing miserably.

Before long, I was laughing with her...and falling closer and closer to fully enthralled.

The smooth skin of her leg under my hand, I leaned forward and touched my lips to hers. They tasted like apple martinis this time, her drink of choice throughout tonight's events, and the buzz in the air was potent.

I needed more than just this kiss, and I needed it badly.

She was like a drug in my veins, and I needed a full hit.

"Are you ready to get out of here?" I asked softly, curling my hand around her neck and my words around the shell of her ear.

She shivered and nodded.

"Yeah," she said, her voice a soft whisper.

I dug out my wallet, tossed down a hundred-dollar bill, and guided her to the coat rack at the front to get our jackets. This wasn't the kind of establishment with a coat check, but at least they'd had a place to put them. The stools at the table would have made the feat difficult.

My fingertips grazed her skin as I slid her jacket up her arms and settled it at her shoulders before leaning forward and burying my face in her hair.

God, she smells good.

After I quickly donned my own coat, we slid out the exit with a nod to the man at the front door and walked the two blocks to my car in near silence.

Tension bloomed and bled between us, and it was all I could do to keep from dragging her down an alley.

As it was, when we made it to the car, I'd waited as long as I could.

With a soft thud, I shoved her into the door and put my lips to hers, and she wrapped her arms around my shoulders in kind.

The build wasn't slow, and the dance of our tongues wasn't subtle. We were both bursting at the seams.

By the time I broke it off, my cock was hard and painful in my jeans, and I pulled my hips away from her to keep her from feeling pressured.

"It was a good night tonight, Gem," I said softly against her neck, trying to get my breathing under control.

"Really good night," she agreed, her voice nothing more than a breath.

I pushed away and opened her door and then clicked it shut behind her when she was safely into the seat.

She watched me the whole way around the hood. I could feel her eyes, but I couldn't watch her.

No, it was safe to say I'd have to spend the entire drive back to her apartment thinking of aunt Alma and her sex toy brigade if I had any hope of calming down my cock.

Chapter Twenty-One

Gemma

Leo pulled up in front of my apartment and slowed the Durango to a soft stop.

Instantly, a whole mess of tingles and flutters filled my belly.

Should I ask him inside?

Does he want to come inside?

I couldn't exactly make assumptions on his behalf, but I knew what I wanted.

And it wasn't a night that ended with a simple good night kiss. But wanting it and not acting like a virgin in a room full of dancing dicks were two different things. In fact, I think I'd proven my track record for being awkward pretty indisputably.

"Do you…uh…want to come in for a…uh…coffee?" I asked, bumbling around my intentions.

Seriously, Gemma? Coffee at midnight?

Leo grinned. "Do you *want* me to come inside for a coffee?"

A quiet chat over coffee was the exact opposite of what I had in mind. And I told him as much. "No, not really."

Of course, my intentions weren't as easy to read in my words as they were in my head, and now I sounded like a wishy-washy person with memory problems.

Not surprisingly, he quirked a brow at my rebuttal. "So, you don't want me to come inside for coffee. But you just asked me to come inside for coffee because…?"

Shit. This sure wasn't going as planned. *Now would be the perfect time to stop beating around the proverbial sex bush and just tell him what you want… Man up, Gemma.*

I looked deep into his baby-blue eyes, let my gaze linger down his face, all the way to his full lips.

Fuck pleasantries. Fuck manners. Fuck Leo—*literally*.

"I asked you to come inside for coffee because, well, I was trying to be super smooth and not so obvious. But in reality, I'm secretly just hoping you'll come inside and get naked," I admitted boldly. As soon as I was done, I had to avert my eyes from the vulnerable way it made me feel, but I'd done it. I was impressed with myself.

Sex-motivated or not, putting yourself out there like that wasn't easy, and I'd taken the chance.

The car went silent for a beat, and when I found the courage to meet his face again, a slow, sexy as fuck smirk curled one corner of his mouth.

"And what will you be doing in this equation?"

You.

Even though inside, my heart was beating against my rib cage, I shrugged off his question like I was all of a sudden cool as a cucumber. *I am confident, I am woman, I am sex goddess.* "I guess it depends."

His smirk grew wider. "On what exactly?"

"On if I like what I see." I shrugged again, and a wolflike laugh left his lips.

It was amused and turned on, and good God, Grandma, the teasing was all the better to foreplay me with. Without pretense or a verbal response, he leaned right in, closer and closer until I could feel the heat of his breath mingling with mine, and then finally, he gave me the sweet relief of contact.

His lips on mine, perfect and pure, and the anticipation in my core bursting in a wild display of fireworks and let's-get-the-fuck-inside.

The kiss turned devious when his tongue snuck past his teeth and gently licked along the seam of my mouth, and when he slipped his tongue in to dance with mine, I moaned.

Okay, who needs the indoors? Streets and cars and steamy windows are where it's at.

It was a curl-my-fucking-toes kind of kiss, and I was more than ready to channel sixteen-year-old Gemma and engage in a hot and heavy make-out sesh in his car.

Evidently, Leo had other plans and started to slow the kiss way, *way* down.

"I think we both know you're going to more than like what you see," he whispered against my mouth as I struggled to be okay with the stopping.

I've mentioned that I'm a doer. A full-motion, on-the-go lady who likes to keep occupied. Well, when it came to kissing men with big hands and skilled tongues and eyes that made the sun seem dull, apparently, all that motivation *to do* turned into an obsession. Do lips. Do tongues. Do *Leo*.

Enthralled with the activities as I was, I had to shake my head at least two times to figure out what he was even answering.

Had I asked something? Suggested something saucily? I couldn't remember. The only balm to my pout was a single final kiss he pressed to my lips like an oral consolation prize.

Still, I full on pouted. I couldn't help it. I wanted more of whatever black voodoo magic he was sending my way. His grin was the only thing that made me feel better about the sudden silence of the engine as he climbed out the door and rounded the hood to open the one on my side for me.

An easy whisk of the door and a helping hand later, my heels hit the concrete for a split second before he lifted me up into his arms in an army hold with a whoosh. I squealed, full-on Justin Belieber at a concert decibel levels.

"Oh my God! What are you doing?"

"Just making sure you get inside safely." He winked and took the steps up toward my apartment two at a fucking time.

"It feels like you're in a hurry," I said through a few giggles, but he ignored me, his strides only increasing in speed until he came to a halt at the entrance.

"Keys?" he asked simply, and I giggled again. Knowing he was suffering as greatly as I was somehow eased my own hissy fit, but that didn't mean I slowed. As quickly as I could, I obliged by reaching inside my purse and unlocking the entry door.

Before I knew it, we were in the main lobby and nearing the elevator at a record-breaking pace.

"Are you sure you're not in some kind of rush?" I asked again, taunting him for my own enjoyment.

No doubt about it, the man had some fucking stamina. My brain started to entertain ideas of what all of that professional football training equated to in the bedroom. I was hoping for a whole lot of *touchdowns.*

"Rush?" he questioned with a devilish smirk. "Not at all."

His actions completely belied his words as, instead of waiting for the always slow as hell elevator in my building, he kicked open the door to the stairs and started jogging up them two at a time.

With me *still* in his arms.

It took all of two minutes before I'd unlocked the door to my apartment and Leo carried me inside.

"You can put me down now, you lunatic," I teased, and thankfully, he set me back to my feet just before shutting and locking my front door.

Luckily, the apartment was still as night, the only sounds filling my ears the steady, pounding beats of my heart and the soft murmurs of Leo's breath behind me.

"Show me your bedroom, Gem," he whispered directly into my ear. His chest was pressed to my back, and I took a hearty inhale through my nose just to savor the delicious smell of him.

Soft yet strong. Woodsy yet clean. He smelled like a goddamn forest mixed with sunshine and vanilla. It was intoxicating.

He was intoxicating.

Without another word, I took his hand in mine and led the way, through the living room, down the short hall, and into my bedroom.

Coffee wasn't on the agenda tonight.

But seeing Leo Landry naked certainly was.

The room was shrouded in twilight and shadows, and it took a minute for my eyes to adjust.

Before I could make my way to the bedside lamp, Leo wrapped his strong arms around my back, and with one gentle pull and a twist, I was in his arms and his blue eyes stared down at me.

His hand moved into my hair, and instantly, goose bumps peppered my skin.

That strong hand slid down my cheekbones to my lips, and his index finger paused for a beat, just barely touching my mouth. "I fucking love these lips," he whispered.

He didn't give me any time to respond.

His lips to mine, the kissing was officially restarted.

Deep. Heady. Urgent. He kissed with purpose, with passion, but also, with this reckless abandon like he couldn't get enough of me.

And his big hands, well, they were *everywhere*.

In my hair. Down my arms. Cupping my breasts. Gripping my ass.

I moaned, and my hips made a bid to fuse with his as I moved closer and pressed my body against his.

I was a fan of whatever Leo was putting down, and we'd yet to take our clothes off. If Leo were a type of alcohol, he'd be a fine fucking wine. Robust and delicious and so damn strong, it went straight to your head.

He sure as hell went straight to my head.

And, good God, our bodies fit together as if we were made to lose ourselves in one another.

Next thing I knew, I was in his arms again as he carried me toward the bed and let me fall onto the mattress with a soft bounce.

I giggled. Leo smirked. And we locked eyes for a moment, just enough for us to feel safe with one another. Just enough for our intense feelings for one another to be validated. Just enough for both of us to understand that what we were feeling was one hundred percent mutual. Just enough to turn this romp from fucking into something *more*.

My breath came out in pants as he undid my jeans and pulled them off, and then he sank to his knees at the bottom of the bed.

He wouldn't be there for long as his mouth followed a line back up, but the sight of him down there for even a moment had my chest ready to explode.

Slowly, he kissed my skin from my toes upward, and his hands were on my legs, always just a little higher than the kisses. My back arched off the bed from the feel of it, from the anticipation, from the overwhelming intensity of it all.

It didn't take long for the rest of my clothes to disappear from my body and Leo's to end up on my bedroom floor. We kissed and we touched and we felt one another, until the mere feeling of our skin moving softly together made me insane with need.

"Now," I whispered and dug my fingers into the bare skin of his back. "Now, Leo," I panted as I ground my hips toward his.

I could feel how aroused he was between my thighs, big and thick and throbbing, and I wanted to know what he felt like inside of me.

Scratch that. I *needed* to know.

Leo sat up on his knees, grabbed his jeans from the floor, and reached into the pocket to pull out a condom. I watched with rapt, fucking riveted attention as he sheathed himself and gave his cock a squeeze at the base as he finished rolling.

He was big and thick and hard in all of the right places. From the tips of his toes to his perfect cock, he looked good naked. Every single blessed inch of him.

I barely blinked as he fell forward and found me swiftly, teasing just the tip inside until he had a good seat and then sliding smooth and slow until he hit the end.

I'd never felt so deliciously full in my entire life.

"You like my cock inside of you, sweetheart?" he whispered. I moaned and nodded as he thrust his hips forward, once, twice, three mind-blowingly deep times.

"Yes," I panted, feeling like the nod and moan needed—no, deserved—the verbal confirmation. He smirked at my enthusiasm just before taking my mouth in another hot and heady kiss, our tongues entwined in an erotic dance.

"Fuck," he muttered and picked up the pace. Each drive forward of his cock timed with that of his tongue inside my mouth. His hands were in constant motion—touching me, feeling me, caressing me.

My breathing turned erratic and my head swirled deliriously, and it didn't take long before I felt my climax build and build and build.

But Leo knew what the fuck he was doing because he didn't let me orgasm right away. *No.* He prolonged it. Slowed it the fuck down and held me right at the glorious edge until I was damn near begging him for release.

I had no idea how much time had passed. It could have been five minutes, or it could have been five hours for all I knew.

But time didn't matter when Leo Landry was fucking your brains out.

When I finally jumped off the proverbial cliff and my orgasm took hold, all rational thought went out the window, and all sorts of incomprehensible moans and words and just fucking sounds left my lips as I felt that orgasm inside every cell of my body.

Leo wasn't far behind me, and when he drove himself in as deep as he could go, a deep, raw, guttural groan escaped his lungs as he emptied himself inside of me.

The world turned fuzzy as my mind reeled over what had just happened, and all I could do was lie in my bed, sex-drunk and still panting to catching my breath.

Fuck, that was the best sex I'd had in God knows how long.

Forever, my mind whispered. *Forever is the word you're looking for.*

A few quiet moments later, I giggled when he rubbed his nose against mine. "Best fucking midnight cup of coffee I've ever had," he teased, and I couldn't not grin. I wasn't a Colombian roast, but apparently I'd hit the spot all the same.

We were mushy and glowing and bound by each other in the connection we still held bodily.

But the rubber band of intimacy snapped with a pop.

Several pops in succession, in fact.

Fucking clapping, for fuck's sake. Raucous and unchecked, it filled my ears from the other side of my door and totally robbed me of my opportunity for an orgasm-fogged witty retort.

"Bravo!" the voice yelled from the hallway. "Brav-fucking-o, you guys!"

It only took two words for me to realize it was Abby.

My not-my-roommate-roommate.

"Seriously!" Abby shouted from what I assumed was the living room. "Great job! I give that sex a ten!"

Leo looked at me with a quirked brow, and I lived in the bloom of the fire-like blush spreading across my skin. After all, with Leo on top of me—with Leo *inside* me—there wasn't exactly a place to hide my head. "I thought you said you didn't have any roommates?"

"I don't." *God, Abby.* My voice was shaky, from both the embarrassment and the orgasm as I tried to explain. "But I do have a best friend who seems to keep forgetting this isn't her apartment."

Leo took it in stride—really, the way he seemed to take everything—a small smile playing at the corner of his lips as he pulled some loose hair out of my face and ran a soft thumb over the flush on my cheek.

I leaned into his touch like a cat preening for pets, and he indulged me.

"Is this the same friend who sent us to Drag on our first date?"

I nodded. "One and the same."

Leo chuckled and rubbed the tip of his nose against mine before speaking a literal breath away from my lips. "Makes sense." I smiled at his easygoing acceptance and melted a little farther into his arms. With a wink and kiss, he spoke against my lips one last time. "I'm just glad she wasn't in your bedroom."

And then he took my mouth in the kind of distraction that would last for a lifetime.

Glad she wasn't in my bedroom? *Me fucking too.*

Maybe, if I was really lucky, she'd rate us even higher for round two.

Chapter Twenty-Two

Leo

The cursor blinked on the screen in the answer box for the fourth time in a half an hour, and I sighed heavily.

I'd been working on this practice quiz for longer than I cared to admit, and the more time that passed, the less I seemed to know.

Graduate-level classes at Rochester Institute of Technology had been more than a whim. In fact, they'd been a careful part of the discussion my parents and I'd had about taking on a career in football.

My success and longevity weren't guaranteed, and as much as they believed in me, they believed even more in the power of a back-up plan. Of course, I hadn't really thought it'd be this hard at the time.

Once I'd been accepted into RIT's Architecture Graduate Program, and had been given a little bit of special treatment through the availability of online courses because of my spot on the Mavericks' roster, I'd decided to take it slow while I was in-season.

Taking one online class at a time couldn't be that hard, I'd thought.

Hah!

What a fucking joke. Online classes were meant to fit into a schedule more flexibly—though, I wasn't sure they were intended for a schedule as packed as mine—but that didn't mean the material was any easier. If anything, it meant I spent ninety percent more time teaching myself the things an in-person professor would have.

And despite my love for architecture, my one and only course—Architectural History—was kicking my ass.

Frustrated, my mind drifted time and time again back to much happier thoughts.

To thoughts of Gemma.

And me.

And a serious lack of clothes.

And how fucking good it'd felt to be inside of her two nights ago.

Consumed by the image of our writhing bodies and sweaty skin, I could picture the two of us together as if it were happening right then. Me over her, her eyes wide at first, and then slowly closing as the power of her orgasm overwhelmed her.

Honestly, it was too goddamn bad my quiz wasn't based on this material.

I'd have been sure to get a fucking A.

One minute drifted into two as I pictured my hands on Gemma's breasts and my mouth following their path.

Soft, pink, perfect nipples and the best-tasting skin I'd ever had the pleasure of sucking on.

God, I'd give anything to have those tits in my mouth now.

Loud and obnoxious, the buzz of my phone against my desk startled me rudely out of my daydream.

My cock was half hard and loaded, ready to go, and when it saw the name Gemma on the screen, it went ahead and jumped to full mast.

"Well, hello," I answered, the gravel in my voice a little too apparent. "I was just thinking about you."

"Dirty things, I presume," she said sweetly, and my dick jerked in my pants.

I bit my lip and gripped my cock with a stern fist to get it under control.

"Maybe," I said innocently. Hoping desperately to come up with something to make myself sound less like a pervert, I glanced to the screen and got an idea. "Really, I was thinking about how smart you are."

"How smart I am?" she asked cautiously, and I laughed a little at her trepidation.

"Yes. The smartest."

"This sounds really suspicious and has taken a turn I didn't expect."

I chuckled. "I'm working on homework, and it's stumping me."

"Homework? You get football homework?"

My laugh was rough and loud as I realized she had no fucking clue about the class at RIT. Football homework. Jesus.

"No, no. I'm taking an online graduate class. I'm doing homework for that."

Gemma was no less than flabbergasted. "A graduate class? Online? Why the hell are you doing that?"

"Well, we didn't really get into it the other night, but as much as my family believes in me, they also believe in a backup plan. And so do I."

"Wow. I'm impressed."

I laughed. "Well, don't be. Right now, I'm sucking at it."

"I'm sure it's not that bad."

"I've been staring at the same question for half an hour."

She sighed, big and beleaguered and dramatic. "Wow. That's pathetic."

"Thanks," I retorted through a laugh. "Your support is astounding."

"Well, I might be willing to help you if you came over here. I mean, I'll at least consider it under the promise to bring food."

"Really?"

"The food part is really important."

I laughed again, jumping up from my spot at my desk and gathering my shit. "I can bring food. Definitely. It'll probably be about an hour before I get there, though."

"Okay," she said easily. "I'll just make some popcorn to hold me over."

And that was that. With a smile and a bounce in my step, I grabbed my stuff and headed for Gemma.

I wasn't sure I'd be able to concentrate on anything but her when I got to her apartment, but I was a good student, after all.

I was certainly willing to give it a try.

Chapter Twenty-Three

Gemma

"Well, hello," I greeted Leo at the door. He wore a black hoodie and a pair of sweats and his hair was still a little damp from a shower, but Lord Almighty, he looked damn fine.

And if my smile would've gotten any bigger, it would've eaten my face.

"Hello, beautiful," he said before placing a sweet kiss on my cheek and walking past.

I didn't hesitate to check out his ass as he headed for my kitchen. Firm and toned in all the right places, it was *bitable.*

In fact, if I had an extra room in my apartment, I'd have been half tempted to create a shrine in its honor. Candles, photos, and just the right amount of creepy lighting to make it believable, it would've looked like a set from *The Craft.*

Which, if you haven't seen the movie The Craft, you are seriously missing out.
Four girls who happen to be witches casting spells on their fellow asshole classmates?

It is every teenage girl's revenge fantasy.
Plus, Skeet Ulrich is a total babe in that movie.
And, seriously, who doesn't love a young Neve Campbell?

Only two official dates and I'd apparently barreled past the point of playing it cool and landed straight in the "I'm crushing on you so bad, and I can't hide it" stage.

Because I was. I was crushing on Leo Landry *hard*.

After he set down his messenger bag on the kitchen table, he held up one large brown paper bag and grinned. "Hungry?"

"If you say there are tacos in that bag, I might get down on one knee and propose marriage."

His responding smile was infectious. "What about the best burgers and fries in Brooklyn? Is the marriage proposal still on the table then?"

Burgers were nice, but I loved *tacos*.

"Nope."

"Damn," he muttered. "Well, feel free to go sit somewhere else while I enjoy these juicy burgers."

"Whoa. Whoa. Whoa," I said and put one defiant hand to my hip. "I never said I wouldn't eat the burgers and fries."

"But what if I don't want to share now?" he asked with a mischievous raise of his brow. "I mean, you got me all amped up for a marriage proposal, and now I'm completely let down."

"Should I remind you that you came over here so that I could help you with grad homework?"

"All right, Gem. I *guess* you can have a burger." Leo grinned and held out the bag toward me.

I snatched it from his hands, and he chuckled as I headed toward the cabinets and started dishing out the food onto actual plates. I might've been a heathen, but I was the kind of heathen who used dishes. Classy as fuck.

As part of my right as the food distributor, I popped a fry into my mouth and moaned. "Oh yeah, that's the good stuff."

"Yet not good enough, apparently," he teased, and I flashed him a roll of my eyes over my shoulder.

"Ketchup? Mustard? Mayo?" I asked and started pulling out the condiment bottles from my fridge.

"Mayo?"

"You've never dipped your fries in mayonnaise before?"

He shook his head. "Um, no."

"Oh my God, you are seriously missing out."

"On a heart attack, maybe. It doesn't matter anyway. By the time you bring the food over here, I'm pretty sure you'll have eaten all of my fries."

"It was just one!" I shouted with an outraged laugh, turning to look at him. "And we're not all health-conscious football stars, Leonard," I snorted. "Some of us enjoy the greasier, junk food things in life from time to time."

"I'm not health-conscious."

I quirked a brow. "You have six-pack abs and the freaking V muscle. Only a squeaky-clean diet and insane workouts can get you those glorious things."

"Glorious things?" he questioned with a devilish grin. "Sounds like you're a fan."

"Shut up and grab the condiment bottles and your homework. We're going to binge in my bed."

"Sounds kinky," he teased, and I sashayed my hips a little as I walked.

"Burgers, fries, *mayonnaise,*" I purred. "Things are about to get all kinds of dirty up in this place."

We settled into my bed, our plates of junk food displayed like a mouthwatering buffet on top of my comforter, and I switched on the television to a rerun of *Live PD.*

"It's crazy the number of people who are never driving their own cars," Leo commented.

"Or wearing their own pants," I added, and he laughed.

"It's always someone else's drugs."

"Always," I agreed, and my eyes went wide with delight when the officers called in the K-9 unit to sniff a guy's car for drugs. "Yesssss!" I exclaimed. "This is my favorite part!"

Leo grinned. "The K-9's?"

"Hell yes! Bring in the K-9's!"

We watched and ate while the cops found a stash of drugs in poor Tommy's car that apparently wasn't Tommy's car. It was his friend's car. A friend for whom he didn't have any information. More of an acquaintance, so to speak. Obviously, Tommy had just borrowed the car and had no idea there were drugs inside.

Not to mention, the crack pipe in his pants also wasn't his.

Poor Tommy was having a real shit night.

But, me? I was having a fabulous fucking night.

All thanks to Leo.

Handsome, playful, hilarious Leo.

The man had my full attention.

Once we finished our food, he pulled his laptop out of his messenger bag, and we dove headfirst into his current assignment.

Surprisingly, not only was Leo a freaking professional football star for the New York Mavericks, but he was also a grad student taking an online course at RIT.

"Explain to me again why you're even busying yourself with school right now?" I asked with a grin. "I mean, isn't football your career? Not to mention, it appears you've done pretty damn well for yourself in that department."

Leo just shrugged. "My career in football isn't guaranteed. One ill-fated injury and it can all be over."

"I guess that makes sense. I mean, it's a little doomsday-ish of a mind-set, but I can understand why you'd want to make sure you have some sort of stable future no matter how it plays out."

"Exactly," he said. "Plus, I've always admired the fact that my dad was a college professor. I mean, his English specialty is a far cry from architecture, but for a long time, I pictured myself following in his footsteps."

"Your dad is a college professor?"

"Was," he corrected. "He retired from his position at NYU about five years ago. My parents are sunning in Florida with the blue hairs now."

I started to respond, and even had a whole bunch of awesome words lined up on the tip of my tongue, but when he reached into his messenger bag and slipped on a pair of reading glasses, I turned stupid.

There was something so incredibly sexy about Leo's baby-blue eyes behind a pair of glasses that it took all of my willpower not to lean forward and do something weird like lick the side of his face.

The view turned me into a dog in heat.

Panting. Drooling. Cartoon eyes. The whole nine fucking yards.

"Gem?" he asked, and I blinked out of my stupor.

"Yeah?"

He grinned. "Am I boring you?"

Boring me? No.

Horny-ing me up with your big muscles and hot nerd glasses? Yes.

"Of course not," I said. "I guess I just zoned out for a minute."

He eyed me knowingly, and I rolled my eyes.

"Fine," I admitted. "Your hot nerd glasses distracted me."

He barked out a laugh. "Hot nerd glasses?"

"Yeah." I nodded toward his face. "Those fucking things should be illegal."

"You got some kind of fantasy with a devastatingly handsome man in glasses, Gem?" he asked and playfully nudged my shoulder with his. "Because I have no issues obliging."

I wished I could have called bullshit on his devastatingly handsome man comment, but let's face it, cocky or not, Leo Landry was exactly that.

"How about we focus on your homework and leave the fantasies for another time?"

"That sounds like a terrible idea."

I playfully rolled my eyes and concentrated on the task at

hand—Leo's current grad assignment, a practice quiz and a twenty-page thesis on the importance of ethics in architecture and original design.

"What are you writing for the thesis?"

He shrugged. "Fuck, if I know."

"Why don't you focus on the ever-growing tension within our world's political climate and how it should be morally and ethically just for governments to be transparent with each other when it comes to infrastructure advancement?"

"Why do you think governments should be transparent with each other?"

"Because no one government owns more than what is within their country's borders," I said. "And whatever is discovered or created could greatly affect more than one country, especially those with high-poverty populations."

Leo searched my eyes for a brief moment, and I felt a bit exposed underneath his gaze.

"What?" I asked. "Why are you looking at me like that?"

"I knew you were intelligent," he said, "but you're really fucking smart, Gem. You do realize that, right?"

"I mean, I know I'm not stupid," I said through a laugh. "I just don't really have my shit together when it comes to knowing what I want to do with my life."

"How long have you been doing temp work?"

"Over a year," I explained. "I started when I dropped out of college my senior year."

"What were you majoring in?"

"I was in the engineering program at NYU."

"That's not an easy program to get into."

"I know." I laughed. "Trust me, I know. But I just couldn't do it. Engineering is my grandfather's and dad's passion, but it's definitely not mine. They're both still pissed at me for dropping out."

"Do you think you'll go back?"

"To college or the engineering program?"

"Either one."

"Honestly, I don't know," I said. "I mean, it's a hard no when it comes to finishing my engineering degree. I just can't fathom a life where I would be that bored and miserable with my career. But going back to college? The jury is still out on that one."

"What interests you?" he asked. "Deep down, what's your passion?"

Music.

I shrugged. "I'm not sure yet."

He glanced across the room at my desk and took in the messy notebooks scrawled with lyrics and the guitar resting against the wall. My pride and joy, work like a dog, save and scrimp for months, love of my life guitar. He looked at it like I did, and my stomach turned over on itself. "Are you sure about that?"

"Obviously, I love music," I said. "But I just don't see it being an actual career for me."

"You know, I've heard you sing, Gem…".

"At a goddamn drag show," I retorted, but he shook his head.

"*And* karaoke. But the location doesn't matter," he said. "Drag show. Street corner. The goddamn bathroom. The only thing that matters is that you're really fucking talented."

"You think so?"

"I know so," he said and set his laptop down beside his hip and got off the bed to grab my guitar.

"What are you doing?"

"Nothing," he said and sat down on the edge of the bed and strummed a few chords and grinned at me. "Will you play me something?"

I shook my head and laughed. "Nice try, Leonard."

"C'mon, Gem," he said. "It's just you and me. No one else. Plus, you already know I love your voice."

"You do?" I asked and he nodded.

"I do."

"What do you want me to play?"

"Anything," he said and handed me my guitar.

"Okay," I said and took a deep breath as I adjusted the guitar in my lap. "I'll play you a little something I've been working on for the past few weeks."

"You write your own music?"

"Sometimes." I shrugged. "When I'm feeling inspired, I guess."

His responding smile was all the confidence I needed, and before I knew it, I was strumming my fingers across my guitar and playing Leo a song I'd yet to title.

It was about a girl who didn't know what she wanted. A girl who was trying to find her place it the world. A girl who was me.

Leo just sat beside me, watching with rapt attention as I sang each word, each verse, and strummed each note with my fingertips.

When I reached the end of the song, nervous butterflies filled my belly as I set my guitar down beside the bed. The scariest part about singing your own songs was that they were a piece of you. Like, you were just handing your soul to someone on a silver platter, without any guarantee they'd accept it with warmth and love.

It was always so terrifying.

I looked at him from beneath my lashes, and I watched as a slow, tender smile kissed his lips.

"And you thought my hot nerd glasses were a distraction," he muttered, and his smile grew wider. "Good God, Gem, you're so fucking beautiful all the time, but when you sing, I can't feel my own body. Everything, everyone...the whole world except for you goes numb. That song was beautiful."

His words hit me straight in the chest, hard and swift and nauseating, if I was perfectly honest.

They were too much. Too intimate. Too real. Too encouraging on something I'd been trying to tell myself wasn't an option for far too long.

Tight-lipped from uncertainty, I had the odd urge to shield my face from his steady gaze.

But Leo didn't need my focus or my words. Instead, he reached out and pulled me into his arms to take what he needed from me himself. "Thank you," he whispered against my mouth. "Thank you for sharing that with me."

"You're welcome," I whispered back. Little did he know, he'd just given me everything I'd never known I'd needed and more. I couldn't stop myself from leaning forward and pressing my lips to his.

Full and warm and soft, his lips were the perfect after-dinner treat.

He responded with fervor, and when his hands went into my hair, I moaned.

He just felt so good. He *always* felt so good.

Before I knew it, we were fused to one another and tumbling back onto my bed.

My clothes, Leo's clothes—they were a meager memory.

Leo Landry was the real deal. And Leo Landry loving me from the inside out? I'd never known a better, more intoxicating feeling in my entire life.

Chapter Twenty-Four

Leo

C am turned up the radio as we pulled away from the party and smashed his hands in rhythm against the steering wheel. I laughed as he sang along to "Walking in Memphis" like a drunk college girl, despite being the sober driver of the evening.

We'd been guests at a charity event, along with a select few others from the team—basically, whatever guys weren't busy—and Cam and I were getting closer by the day.

I'd never have imagined I could be such good friends with a guy like him—that I'd have stuff in common with someone so much older than me—but it became clearer every day that this would be the kind of friendship that lasted a lifetime.

The offbeat, off-key, god-awful sound of his voice only reminded me of the sweetness of Gemma's, and when he finished belting out the chorus, I reached out to turn the volume knob back down to human levels.

He grumbled good-naturedly, but I dove right into conversation to take some of the sting out of the offense.

"So, how long have you known that Will Chambers guy?"

"Will? The manager at Monarchy?"

I nodded. We'd met him earlier that evening while mingling with the crowd, and Cam was chummy from the get-go. It was obvious they'd crossed paths more than a time or two, and Monarchy was one of the hottest stage-bearing clubs in Manhattan. From what I'd heard, even Ellie Goulding had performed there before becoming famous.

"Yeah."

"I've known him four or five years, I guess. We used to hang out together when we dated girls who were friends."

I nodded along graciously, like I cared, careful to put off getting to the point until I buttered him up.

"Oh, that's cool. Seems like a nice guy. Club is really popular too."

Cam, of course, smelled my bullshit a mile away.

"The best." He smiled, looking back and forth between me and the road as he waited for me to get to the point. When my carefully crafted I'm-not-after-anything smile went on for too long, he laughed and took over leading the conversation again. "You want me to set you up on a date with him or something? Christ, your questions and the seriously creepy look on your face are freaking me out a little bit."

I laughed and sighed, shaking my head before looking out the window and then back to Cam. "No. I just…"

Shit, was I really going to admit to all this? Test our relatively new friendship by asking for a favor for my girlfriend?

This could be such a big deal for Gemma.

Yes. Yes, I was.

"Do you remember Gemma?"

He hummed and drummed his fingertips on the steering wheel as he pretended to contemplate it. "Hmm. Not your Nonnie. Or Nonna. Or what the fuck ever. Blond or something, if I'm remembering correctly." I rolled my eyes, and he scoffed. "Duh. The apple of your eye, dude. The dip to your wick."

I laughed at his crudeness, but he went on anyway.

"Yeah. I remember your girl. Everything still going well with her?"

I nodded at the understatement of the century and locked my

muscles to keep from spewing twenty minutes' worth of compliments and lovey-dovey bullshit. Cam was patient and he was kind, but no amount of bribery in the world would keep him from sharing my love poetry word vomit with Sean if I gave him the material.

"Really well. Couldn't be going any better, honestly."

"What the fuck?" Cam yelled. "And you haven't shared more details? What are we? Acquaintances? You should be telling me everything."

"Well. Sorry," I said with a laugh. "I didn't think you'd want every single detail of my love life."

"Only the interesting ones. The boring shit, you can keep to yourself."

"Yeah." I laughed, knowing good and well I'd be keeping the majority of it to myself no matter what he said. Friendship was great and all, but with a group of guys like them just waiting to peck over my carcass, privacy was even better. Still, this wanting to know more shit kind of played into my hands, so I used it to my advantage. "Okay, well…" I said slowly, "she can really fucking sing."

"Ah," Cam breathed. "Now I'm getting it. She's hounding you, trying to use your connections."

His insinuation caught me completely off guard, and I jerked my head. "What? No! She has no idea that I know anyone or ever would. She's just good. And well, after meeting him tonight, I figured…"

"You just figured your buddy Cam could hook you up," he finished for me with an indulgent smile. I figured he'd be quick to pick up on my motives, but at least he didn't seem angry or annoyed.

"Yeah," I admitted with a shrug of my shoulders.

"Say no more," he said swiftly, pulling up the voice command screen in his truck. "I'll call him right now."

"Really?"

"Yeah," he said with a laugh and called out Will Chambers to the voice command. As the phone started to ring, my stomach churned. "You just better hope it's not your fucking hormones or dick making her sound good. If you get her a gig at Monarchy, she better be able to really fucking sing."

"She can," I said confidently. This was a big deal, I knew, but Gemma's voice had the rawest, realest talent I'd ever heard in my life. There was no way she would let anyone down if I got her the opportunity.

Cam's schmoozing was fast and effective, and before I knew it, he'd sweet-talked Gemma right into a prime position on Monarchy's stage next week. My body buzzed with the excitement at how quickly it was all coming together.

Gemma's passion for music mirrored my passion for football. It ran through her veins and stayed intertwined with her soul. It was who she was. And it was exactly what she should be doing.

I only wanted good things for my girl.

And this opportunity, it was all the good things.

It was a huge fucking deal.

When Cam dropped me off at my place, I went straight to my Durango and fired it up before giving her a call.

This late at night, I didn't want to show up without notice, but the reason? Well, that was worthy of a surprise.

I had the best news ever. I could *not* wait to tell her.

And by telling her in person, when the initial celebration was over, we'd have the whole rest of the night to celebrate in even better ways.

Chapter Twenty-Five

Gemma

"I'm sorry, you did what?" I asked, the roar of blood in my ears making it impossible to tell if I'd actually heard what I thought I had.

He was so happy, so fucking enthusiastic, and I was…trying not to throw up. I'd heard the lilt in his voice, the glee in his tone, the pure excitement in his every word when he called, but I'd naïvely thought…I don't even know. I guess I'd just thought he was like every man I'd ever engaged with biologically, and that he was just really, truly animated about having sex.

When he'd said he was on his way, I'd turned giddy.

I'd taken a quick shower and gotten so fresh and so clean and even put on my sexiest pair of lace panties beneath my cutest pajamas.

I'd had it all worked out in my mind.

I'd answer the door.

Smiles would occur.

Then Leo would walk inside, and we'd live up to the two-a.m. booty call hype.

I'd never thought it'd be…this.

Good God, what had he done?

"I booked you a gig at Monarchy," Leo repeated, the exact words I was really hoping I'd misheard taunting me through each and every syllable. "Cam knows the guy in charge of booking acts—"

My heart woke the fuck up at his words and started pounding against my ribs like a hammer. I didn't have the tact or care to stop myself from interrupting.

"You booked me a gig?"

"I did." He grinned and bounced on his toes and nodded with pride as I grew a little greener. Part of me didn't want to believe it was as bad as I could be making it out to be, so I stalled, hoping when I asked for the details I prayed weren't true, he'd set me free from this hell.

"Monarchy? As in one of *the* most popular nightclubs in Manhattan?"

"Yep."

I glanced around my living room manically, trying to focus on something, *anything*, to slow my heart, but the walls of my apartment were starting to close in around me. I was suffocating—drowning—*dying* at the very real certainty that he'd pushed me off a cliff I'd been scrambling away from for over a year.

"Isn't it awesome?"

Instead of answering him, I had to sit down on my couch before my knees buckled out from under me.

He'd somehow, someway, booked me a fucking gig at one of the biggest nightclubs in the city.

Drag shows, karaoke bars, hell, even open mic nights with all of thirty people in the crowd were one thing, but an actual gig like this? A goddamn nightclub packed to the gills? Fuck, I wasn't ready.

I wasn't ready to be judged by all those people, and I wasn't ready to even entertain the idea of music as something more than a hobby.

My parents—my grandfather—they would *never* be on board. I could be the next fucking finalist on *American Idol,* and they'd still tell me music was a pipe dream.

"Gem?" Leo asked and sat down beside me. "Are you okay?"

Around and around, my mind spun on the turmoil that would take over my family for years if I let myself do this…if I let myself get my hopes up. If I gave my everything to making it a career and… God, what if I failed?

If I put myself out there…if I sang my words, my lyrics…if I played my riffs, my notes, my music…what if I did all of that and didn't get the warm, open-armed reaction I craved?

What if I threw my relationship with everyone I'd ever had my whole life out the window for *nothing?*

I knew my parents and my grandpa didn't need to know about one performance, but what if one performance led to two, which led to three…which led to me attempting a career with music?

They'd disown me.

And fuck, what if they disowned me *and* I failed?

Anxiety burrowed itself in my chest, and I tried like hell to breathe through the choking sensation that had taken up residence in my throat.

"What's going on, sweetheart?"

Leo's concern was growing by the minute, but I clearly didn't know what to say. So, I stared down at my hands that were now tightly clenched together in my lap. How did I even begin to broach turning him down without him making a big deal about it?

He'd been encouraging my music every time we were together, and he wouldn't understand my rejecting this.

Hah. By the amount of excitement he'd bled all over my front door when he'd arrived, I could tell he wouldn't understand *at all.*

"Gem?" Leo whispered my name, and I looked up from my hands and into his baby-blue eyes. "You all right?"

"No," I answered honestly, finally finding it in me to make something other than my mind move. "I'm not all right."

He searched my eyes and I knew it was my responsibility to tell him how I was feeling, but navigating this complicated of an issue felt like wading through water full of sharks.

"Leo…why did you book a gig for me?"

He reached out and took my hand in his. "Because you're so fucking talented, baby. It's so obvious that music is your passion, and it's what you're meant to do, Gem. And it's time you start actually doing it."

Sick with tension, I tried to hold myself removed from his hype, to make it clear that he needed to back off, without being hurtful. The last thing I wanted to do was turn this into something between the two of us.

I just didn't know if it was avoidable.

"But that's not your decision to make," I said through a firm jaw. "That's my decision."

He tilted his head to the side and searched my face. "You're not happy about this?"

"No," I answered simply. "I'm not happy about this, Leo. This is such a bigger issue than I can explain, and the fact that you didn't talk to me about this first... I just... I don't know what to think right now."

"You're mad at me?" he asked, and shock rang out in his voice like a bell. "You're seriously mad at me for getting you an opportunity like this?"

"An opportunity?" I spat back. "An opportunity for what, Leo? Fucking failure? Dissention in my family?"

"You're not going to fail, Gem," he said. "And your family will understand. When they see how brilliant you are, they'll understand!" He tried to hold my hand again, but I snatched it away.

"How would you know?" I asked, and my voice continued to rise with irritation. "You don't know anything about this. You don't know what it's like with my parents and my grandfather. You don't know that they'll understand because you don't know them. They're not your family, Leo. It's not that simple!"

"Gem," he said, but I just shook my head and stood up from the couch. I didn't want to fight with him. It was the last fucking thing on the planet I wanted. He'd quickly become the brightest spot in my life and the only thing I had left that I felt like I'd done right.

I couldn't do this anymore tonight without ruining it. If we kept going, I would say something I would regret—we would regret—forever. I just knew it.

"I'm tired, Leo," I said. "I think it's a good idea if we just call it a night."

"You're kicking me out?" he asked, and I shook my head. That wasn't the way it was, but I knew that was the way he would see it no matter what I said or did. I just didn't have the energy to make sure he knew the difference.

"Right now, I think it's best if you just give me some space."

"Space?" he questioned, and his jaw tightened with his words. "You want space from me?"

"Yeah, I do. For tonight. I need it."

"Wow," he muttered and ran a hand through his hair before eventually standing. "Well, by all means, let me give you your space," he added before heading toward the door. Anger lined the top of his shoulders, and a cold chill crept up my spine. "Good night, Gem," he tossed haphazardly over his shoulder just before he walked out of my apartment.

Tears threatened, and anger quickly made an appearance in an attempt to distract me. How in the hell had any of this even happened?

It felt like one minute, I'd been excited about Leo coming over and putting on my sexiest pair of lace panties, and the next, I'd told him I needed space and he'd all but stormed out of my apartment.

Stunned, I walked into my kitchen and opened the fridge to snag a bottle of water from the bottom shelf.

I twisted open the cap, and just before I lifted it to my lips for a long drink, the living room window that led to the fire escape creaked open, and my already aching heart all but jumped out of my throat and onto the damn floor.

The curtains shifted, and my lungs tightened in fear as I prepared to see the face of a serial killer or ax murderer, but when Abby's head peeked through, it took all of my willpower not to toss the water bottle at her head.

"What the fuck?" I questioned and put a shaking hand to my chest. "What are you doing on the goddamn fire escape?"

"Just getting some fresh air." She shrugged and shut the window with a rattle behind her after climbing inside. "And, unfortunately, overhearing you being a huge bitch to your boyfriend."

"I wasn't being a bitch," I denied, but the words felt like a lie even as they left my lips. I hadn't *meant* to be a bitch. She rolled her eyes and plopped down onto my couch.

"Um, yes," she retorted. "You were."

"He booked me a fucking gig at Monarchy, Abby," I said by way of explanation, knowing the rest of the details were important but too tired to get into them. "Without even talking to me first."

"Oh man," she said, and sarcasm dripped from her voice. "How awful that your boyfriend would book you a gig at one of the biggest clubs in the city because he thinks you're super talented and wants to help you live your passion. What a bastard."

Her words were a punch to the gut chock-full of perspective. Leo wasn't the bad guy here. I was. My family's expectations weren't his fault, and my battle to keep a relationship with them wasn't his responsibility. He'd done something genuine for me out of the kindness of his heart, and I'd essentially thrown it in his face. I stood frozen in my spot.

"He just wants to help you, Gem," Abby added, but this time, she dropped the sarcasm and settled for soft and gentle. "He believes in you like I believe in you."

He believed in me like my own family didn't.

And I fucked it up.

How in the hell was I going to fix it?

Chapter Twenty-Six

Leo

To say I wasn't in the clearest headspace during our sixth game of the season would be an understatement.

Gemma's and my fight weighed heavily on my mind and took up residence in my limbs, and for a guy who was supposed to chase big, muscled dudes for an hour's worth of playing time—and keep up with them—that wasn't a good thing.

All I could do was be thankful that I hadn't fucked up royally and screwed up our current winning record *and* chances at the championship.

No doubt if I had, I'd have more than Gemma mad at me.

Frustration was ripe as I ripped off my pads to the sounds of celebration around me.

A win was a win.

It didn't matter to the other guys what fucked-up things were going on in my head, and quite frankly, I was glad. I didn't need any of them trying to play shrink with my love life.

Or lack of love life, I thought sardonically.

"Hey, Landry," Cam called as he strutted across the locker room.

I jerked up my chin in greeting, but other than that, went about the business of disrobing angrily.

"You were slow as shit out there," he said with a smile, clearly not reading the situation correctly about how frustrated I was.

Or hell, maybe he had.

Maybe he just didn't care.

Still, I didn't hold back as I snapped, "I'm in no fucking mood, Cam."

"Ooh," he cooed, bouncing on his toes and swinging a leg over the bench to take a seat. "Something tells me all is not well in paradise."

"Shut up," I barked.

"Wow. Like, really not well."

"Cam."

"Okay, okay, I'll lay off. Only because you didn't completely suck. But trust, son, you start fucking up our record, and I'll be gunning for you."

I took a deep breath to calm myself down and nodded. That was fair, if a little insensitive, and it was the way of the professional football world. It wasn't like high school, where getting dumped by your girlfriend was a valid fucking excuse.

This was the big leagues. This was my job.

This was important to more than just me, and there was a fuck of a lot on the line that the organization wouldn't happily sacrifice to the well-being of my emotions.

It didn't matter that Gem and I had had a fight three nights ago that had kept me from going to sleep. It didn't matter that I'd spent every waking moment at the stadium trying to tune it all out. It didn't matter that she hadn't called since.

Fuck. It mattered.

It just didn't matter to the Mavericks.

Cam gave me a shove, but he lowered his voice before walking away. "For what it's worth, I hope it works out."

I appreciated the kindness, something I knew he didn't have to show me, no matter our friendship. We were relatively new friends in the scheme of things, and in the end, we were colleagues. He'd been working toward a championship for more years than I could fathom, and I couldn't imagine my emotional distress would be a great comfort to him if I somehow fucked it up. "Thanks."

"Now, cheer up. We won. Turn that fucking frown upside down."

I took a deep breath and nodded again, this time letting my face break its pattern enough to form a small smile. He was right. I didn't have to be Mary fucking Poppins, but we were six and oh, and in professional football, that really meant something. Every week, you played a top opponent. Every week, that flawless record was on the line.

If I couldn't find the positives in the showing I'd made during my debut year in *this* league, I couldn't find the positive in anything.

After a quick shower, I gathered my shit and made my way out of the locker room and into the hall. The area was mostly empty, and the rest of the guys were pretty much long gone, already headed out to celebrate, thanks to their lack of need to pout.

I put my head down and steadied myself for the onslaught of reporters that would be waiting outside. So dedicated was my newfound focus to avoiding every-fucking-one, I almost didn't see her as I made to walk by.

"Leo," she called simply—hesitantly.

I *knew* that voice, and never, in my whole life, could I forget that voice.

I mean, it'd only been haunting me for the past three days.

Honestly, it'd been haunting me since the first time I'd heard it all those months ago.

I pulled up short and turned back, squinting into the darkness to see all the hallmarks come to life.

Blond hair.

Killer body.

Sweet blue eyes.

It was her, all right, gilded within the shadow of the dark hallway or not. My emotions weren't playing tricks on me.

"Gemma?"

"Ha. Yeah. It's me," she said and worried her teeth against her lip.

"How'd you get back here?" I asked, knowing the security to get into the hallway with the players was Fort Knox kind of tight.

"I, uh, kind of told the security guard I was your sister and I had your medication."

I narrowed my eyes. "And he believed you?"

She shook her head. "Not even a little. But I think he felt bad for me. Maybe it was the pathetic pout or the black circles under my eyes, but I think it was clear I haven't slept properly for a few days."

I tilted my head with a little laugh and made a note to watch out for psychopaths. Apparently, the security around here wasn't as tight as I'd once thought.

"What are you doing here?" I asked, going straight for the question that mattered.

She nodded then, shuffling her feet slightly and self-consciously. Gone was the vibrant woman I'd brought out to drag clubs and karaoke bars, and back was the one who'd been nervous even to look at me. I hated seeing her like this, but seeing her in general? I didn't hate that at all.

"Yeah, I can see why'd you'd ask that. Abby says I was a bitch to you."

"Abby?"

She laughed. "Yeah. Big shock." Her shoulders bumped up and dropped again in a shrug. "She apparently heard our fight."

I shook my head at her crazy friend and set it aside. Abby wasn't what mattered, as weird as her behavior was. What mattered was the shit that had gone down between Gemma and me. The absolute wrong move I'd made—and the shitty way she'd handled it.

I knew, when it came to our first official fight, we'd both been in the wrong.

I should've talked to her first before booking that gig.

And she should have tried to understand the only reason I'd done it was because I was fucking crazy about her and I only wanted the best for her. Instead, she'd pushed me away and let me go three days of thinking the absolute fucking worst.

"What do you think?" I asked. "Were you a bitch?"

She flinched at my use of the word in the context of her, but in the end, she shrugged. "I was upset. And I know I didn't handle it well, nor did you deserve that kind of awful reaction. Truthfully, I would have gotten in touch sooner, but...I knew it had to be in person. And you're really hard to keep up with this late in the week."

I nodded. Game weeks were always a push in preparation. If she'd have called, I would have answered, but it didn't feel right to put any more blame on her than there already was.

"What did I deserve?"

She smirked. "A polite decline?"

I laughed, relieved to have just a hint of her cuteness back. "And what else?"

"A hug?"

Stepping closer, I pulled her body against mine and pushed us both against the wall. The contact soothed my entire body immediately. "And what else?" I asked again, this time much more softly.

"Hmm. A kiss?"

Leaning forward, I took her mouth with mine and swept my tongue inside. She gasped as it united with hers, and my gut finally unclenched.

Hours, days of agony, all released at once.

Quickly and discreetly, I stepped back and grabbed her hand before guiding her down the hall and behind a door that read Service Closet.

She smiled as we stepped inside, but I didn't give her time to blush, even loving it as much as I did. Instead, I pushed the door shut and her up against it, pulling a leg up onto my hip and pressing our lips together again.

One kiss, two, I worked her mouth and then her neck and all the way down to her collarbone before coming up for air.

"I missed you," I breathed into the little hollow spot at the center, and her hips pushed up and out toward mine.

"Me too," she gasped as I ripped open the buttons of her shirt and put my mouth to the lace of her bra.

Delicately, one nipple at a time, I sucked and plundered until she was writhing against me in agony.

A feeling that maybe slightly resembled the one I'd been carrying around since we parted ways three nights ago.

I worked my way down her body slowly, inch by inch, until I reached the button of her pants, and I didn't stop there. With a quick flick, I undid the button and slid them down her legs, taking the panties with them as I went.

She moaned as the cold air hit her hot, wet clit, and I licked my lips at the sight of her glistening.

"Don't worry, Gem," I said with a wink as I looked up between her legs. "I'll handle this performance all on my own."

She laughed at my audacity, but I didn't.

I got a taste of just the medicine I needed.

And God, did she taste good.

Fuck yes, all is right with the world again.

This beautiful woman, she was everything I wanted and more. So much so that going three days feeling like things had ended between us was not something I ever planned on repeating again.

She was *my* girl. My bombshell mystery package that only I had the pleasure of unwrapping.

Mine to kiss. Mine to hold. Mine to *taste.*

I sucked and ate at her wet pussy, and when I felt her orgasm vibrate against my tongue, I grinned like a greedy fucking bastard. When it came to Gem, all I could think was *mine, mine, mine.*

"Fuck," she whispered once the fog of her orgasm cleared from her mind. "I'm pretty sure I've never come that quick in my life. I feel like I just got hit by an actual orgasm train."

I smirked, made her squeal with one final, gentle lick to her clit, and slid her panties and pants back into place.

She didn't know this yet, but that wouldn't be the only time the supposed *orgasm train* made a stop at her house this evening.

"Ready, Gem?" I asked, and she tilted her head to the side.

"For what?"

"To go home."

"My place or your place?" she asked and I grinned.

"I'd prefer not to have an audience tonight."

"Your place it is," she agreed on a giggle, and I wrapped my arm around her shoulders and led her out of the service closet and into the main hallway.

When she grinned up at me with those pretty blue eyes of hers, my heart swelled.

And right then, right there, I decided.

I wasn't going to let her go.

Chapter Twenty-Seven

Gemma

My phone buzzed inside my pocket, and I set down the package in my hands to check my messages.

Leo: What are you doing, baby?

I quickly typed out a response that made me grin.

Me: Packing up all of your Nonna's dildos... Taking pictures of her thongs... You know, the usual weekday responsibilities.

Leo: Christ, you're never going to let me forget that disturbing reality, are you?

Me: Not likely. ;) What are you doing?

Leo: Thinking about you.

He was sweet, really, he was, but he was also a dirty little liar.

Me: That's real nice, Leonard. But considering I know you're in the middle of practice right now, I'm calling bullshit.

Leo: Fine. I'm thinking about you AND practice. But mostly, thinking about you.

Me: What exactly are you thinking about when you're thinking about me?

His response came not even a minute later.

Leo: Your eyes. Your lips. Your angelic voice. Your pretty little smile. Every-fucking-thing that is Gemma Holden.

He was charming, I'd give him that much.
And his words, well, they made me blush to my damn toes.

Leo: And, if I'm being really honest, I was just recalling the exact moment I decided I was Gemma's number one fan.

Me: Sounds like quite the moment...

Leo: Ironically, it was inside a supply closet, of all places.

Making up for the disastrous misunderstanding we'd had over the gig at Monarchy had been one of the highlights in my spank bank reel ever since. If for nothing else, I figured the fantasies associated with that day had made the fight worth it.

That fight, our first official fight, had been over two months ago, and thankfully, Leo and I had been back in business ever since.

Constant flirtatious banter through texts and phone calls and FaceTime.

Date nights whenever we could fit them in.

Frequent sleepovers.

Lots and lots of fan-fucking-tastic sex.

Yeah. Life was officially good.

And with everything smooth between us, we'd turned our focus back toward outside enemies.

For him, it was a flawless football season and the chance at the championship game—something every team was desperate to dismantle every time they had a game—and for me, it was peddling dildos with Alma.

Well, not that Alma was my enemy, but she sure as shit had the power to be a thorn in my side when she was feeling extra bossy.

It was safe to say my temporary three-month gig at Alma's Secrets had been extended for an un-set amount of time.

Personally, I thought it was because she liked the company *and* the fact that I carried most of the workload.

Eventually, I texted Leo back, a smile tipping up the corners of my lips when I let my mind linger on memories of him and me inside a supply closet in Mavericks Stadium.

Me: I remember that moment. It's my favorite.

Leo: Me too, baby. Me too.

Before I could respond with heart eyes or a kissy face emoji, another text came through.

Leo: Shit. I've gotta get back to practice, but I'll call you after, okay?

Me: Sounds good. I'll just be here packing up all of Nonna's sex toys.

Leo: Goddammit, Gemma.

I giggled and typed out one final message that I knew would

probably make him roll his eyes *and* smile.

Me: Have an awesome practice, baby!

I slid my phone back into my pocket, and it took a good five minutes to swipe the real-life heart eyes from my face.

But, eventually, I refocused on my workday priorities.

Alma and I had been hard at work for most of the morning. Well, when I said *we'd* been hard at work, I really meant me. She'd mostly just been gabbing in my ear and *acting* like she was working on her laptop.

I called bullshit, though.

Every damn time I walked past her screen, I found her messaging with her friend Marty on Facebook or watching pirated reruns of Dr. Phil on YouTube.

By the time the clock had struck noon, I'd barreled through over fifty inventory photos and managed to package up all of yesterday's orders.

With me running the pleasure ship, Alma's Secrets had never been more on top of shit than we were right now.

Funny how I'd never been good at any of my temp jobs until I found one where I stroked dildos all day.

I tossed the last package into the plastic bin I'd managed to talk the guy at the post office into giving me and plopped my ass down into one of the plastic-covered dining chairs. It squeaked as I adjusted in my seat, and Alma slipped off her reading glasses and let out a deep breath.

"We've been two busy bees all day, huh?"

"Well, *I've* been busy," I answered with a knowing smirk. "But I'm not sure your three hours' worth of Dr. Phil videos on YouTube counts."

She grinned. "In my defense, that man would wear anyone out with his psychoanalyzing drivel."

I laughed at that. "Then why do you watch him?"

"Because he's entertaining," she said through a giggle. "Plus, I've always had a thing for bald men."

"You're ridiculous."

"And hungry," she added and shut her laptop. "Time for lunch?"

Right on cue, my stomach growled its agreement, and I nodded. "You want to eat here or head to the diner?"

"Let's eat here," she said and stood up from her seat. "I just made a fresh batch of pasta salad last night, and I've got enough lunch meat to feed Leonard's football team."

I grinned. Alma's pasta salad was legend. I didn't think her theory about standing up to feeding the entire team had truly been tested, but I also didn't think she was wrong. It was carb-loaded, one hundred percent guilty goodness.

"Sounds good."

I followed her into the kitchen and helped set the table while she dished out the food. It didn't take long, even for a slow little old lady, and within ten minutes, we were sitting across from each other and chowing down on turkey sandwiches, potato chips, and Alma's homemade pasta salad.

Colorful penne, veggies, a little cheese, and some kind of Italian dressing and seasonings, it was hands down the best pasta salad I'd ever tasted in my life.

"I want this recipe," I said and popped a forkful of penne into my mouth.

"That's nice, dear, but you can't have it."

"What? Why not?"

She grinned. "Because it's a *secret* recipe."

"What do you mean, it's a secret?"

"I've never given that recipe to anyone. Not even my sister Darla."

A guffaw mixed with a laugh as I judged her aloud. "Well, that's a bit selfish, don't you think?"

A soft laugh left her lips. "If Darla were still alive, she'd definitely agree with that. But I don't care. It's *my* recipe, and I do what I want with it."

God, she was a trip. Ornery as hell, but entertaining nonetheless.

Foiled from adding a recipe to my *very* slim roster, I just grinned and savored the secret pasta. I'd learned since I'd started working for Alma that there was no use arguing with her. And there sure as shit wasn't any way to convince her otherwise. The old biddy was set in her ways, and there wasn't a single man, woman, or child on this earth who could change her. Luckily, even after I was done working for her, I had a feeling anytime I wanted her pasta, all I'd have to do was give her a call and come on over.

"So," she said after taking a bite of her sandwich. "How are things going between you and Leonard?"

Leonard. I loved how she always called Leo by his full first name. Hell, sometimes I found myself doing it too just to tease him.

I shrugged. "They're going pretty good, I guess."

"You guess?" she asked. "What is that supposed to mean?"

Christ, she didn't miss a beat.

"It means I can't predict the future, but right now, things are good."

"How good?" she asked with a little smile perking up her mouth.

"You do realize it's awkward talking to you about Leo, right?" I asked, and she waved a hand in the air.

"Oh, don't be so uptight, Gemma," she retorted. "I'm an eighty-year-old woman who sells sex toys and lingerie, for fuck's sake. Pretty sure I can handle whatever you tell me."

I laughed at that. "Good to know."

"That's it?" she asked. "Good to know?"

I shrugged. "What else do you want me to say?"

"I want you to fess up and tell me how things are really going between you and my nephew," she said without hesitation or shame. "I know you've been spending a lot of time together. Would you say things are getting more serious?"

I honestly didn't know the answer to that question.

Yes, we'd reached a point where we used cute terms of endearment and shit.

And, no doubt, we'd been spending practically all of our free time together.

But Leo and I had yet to have any sort of deep discussion about where we were headed. Mind you, we weren't dating or sleeping with other people, but for the most part, we were just kind of going with the flow.

If I was being honest with myself, deep down, I had a hard time wrapping my head around how polar opposite our lives were.

He was a professional football star for the New York freaking Mavericks.

And I was the temp who took inventory photos for Alma's Secrets.

It might have just been my insecurities talking, but the scale felt a little skewed with him at the very tip-top and me plummeting straight for the bottom.

After we'd made up from the big fight, we'd both just kind of been riding the rails along with the train. I had a feeling neither one of us wanted to veer off track. "I mean, we're not talking about marriage and kids, but things are going good."

"What about the sex?" she asked bluntly, and I nearly choked on my turkey sandwich.

"What in the hell do you mean by that?"

"Is it good? Bad? Just mediocre?" she questioned with a little smirk.

"Things are good, okay?" I said by way of ending this discussion before it got out of hand. "That's all you need to know. Things between Leo and me are good."

She winked. "So, what you're saying is, the sex is good?"

I snorted. "I'm saying there's no way in hell I'm going to answer that question in the disturbing detail you're hoping for."

"Rats," she muttered with an amused smile, and I just giggled.

Our conversation turned quiet for a few peaceful moments until Alma couldn't stand the silence and resumed her chattering ways.

"I have an extra ticket," she said and popped a potato chip into her mouth.

"An extra ticket?"

"To the play-off game in Pittsburgh."

"Oh, who are you planning on taking?" I asked dumbly. Of course. The instant the words left my mouth, I knew I was in trouble.

"I'm going to take you," she said and then added, "Well, technically, you'll be the one taking me, but same difference."

I quirked a brow. "But what if I don't want to go?"

She grinned. "Oh, c'mon, Gemma. I might be old as dirt, but I wasn't born yesterday. Plus, we both know you want to go support the incredibly handsome man in your life."

The old biddy had a point.

"Where is the play-off game again?"

"Pittsburgh."

"But that's like a five-hour drive...."

"Even more reason to have you come along so I don't have to do that long-as-hell trip by myself."

What could I say to that? The mere idea of Alma making the long drive by herself made me instantly nervous.

Plus, I really, really wanted to see Leo's play-off game.

Even though I might regret being stuck inside a car with Alma for five hours, the decision was pretty damn obvious.

"Okay," I said. "Let's go to Pittsburgh together."

Chapter Twenty-Eight

Leo

Our first play-off game was intense, and the crowd was on its feet. It'd been a madhouse of over one-hundred-decibel noise nearly the entire time we were playing, and I'd had to turn myself into a goddamn werewolf to hear Quinn call the plays.

But if shapeshifting was ever going to be worth it, I figured it was when we had so much on the line and a championship run still alive.

I could feel the sweat running all over my body despite the frigid Pittsburgh winter air, and Sean had been in full hype mode on the sidelines for an entire hour and a half. Waving his arms, jumping up and down, catcalling like a psychopath, he'd demanded our crowd get to their feet and do their part, and they hadn't fallen down even a little bit.

Because of the overwhelming intensity pouring down around us, and the focus I'd been honing with a fine laser since we'd stepped out onto the field, I didn't notice Gemma and Alma up in the stands until sometime during the fourth quarter when Cam had given me a nudge and pointed them out.

Apparently, according to him, they'd been raising enough hell together in the stands to get his attention. Considering I could barely hear myself think, let alone pick out two individuals without a strong reason in that mess, they must have been pretty fucking loud.

I'd given a quick jerk of a nod before getting back to focusing, but with the way Cam the puppy dog wouldn't leave me alone as I finished putting all of my dirty shit in my bag after my shower, I'd say he hadn't done the same.

"Come onnnn, dude. I want to meet them."

He'd been relentless since even before the end of the game, and it'd been all I could do to tune him out and keep my head on the field. It was the first time Gemma had been there in the stands to see me play and the first time for my Nonna all season. Maybe it wasn't a big deal to Cam to split his attention between them and football, but I'd known if I'd let myself go down their road for even a minute, I'd have been fucked and we might have lost.

And he'd be feeling a lot differently right now.

I rolled my eyes. "I'm almost ready. Why are you rushing me? Isn't Lana around?"

He pouted. "No. She couldn't come. She had to work."

"So, I'm your toy?"

He shook his head laughingly. "Nope. But your girl and the old lady are. I cannot wait to meet them. You should have seen the shit they were doing in the stands. I thought your girl was going to take off her shirt if it took me much longer to spot them."

I rolled my eyes. I might have freaked out if I believed him for even a second. But Gemma wasn't the type to take off her top at a football game, desperate for attention or not. "Her name is Gemma. And the old lady is my aunt Alma."

"Alma, huh?"

I laughed, warning, "You better watch her. Give her attitude, and she'll have you eating shit for breakfast."

He smiled hugely and laughed. "Feisty. I love it. It's my favorite quality in a lady."

"You have no idea," I admitted. Hopefully, she would give Cam a run for his money and then some. It might be nice to see him suffer a little bit.

I'd yet to confront her about her sex toy business since Gemma
had broken the news, and I didn't think I ever would. Still, just knowing made all the sense in the world.

Nonna was one of a kind, and she didn't take crap from anyone.

I couldn't imagine sex toys had been widely accepted in her time,
but if there was ever a woman not to give a fuck, it was her.

"All right," I said, swinging my bag onto my shoulder. "I'm ready."

My excitement to see the two of them was almost overwhelming,
but I'd forced myself to keep it in check because I knew I wouldn't be
able to stay with them. I never minded the rules of the team—*you
come as a team, you leave as a team*—but I'd never had my two favorite people in the world come to an away game before.

Cam, on the other hand, didn't try to contain his jubilation at all.
He jumped up and down like a schoolgirl. "It's about time."

"Can you calm down?" I asked with a laugh. "If they meet you
like this, they're going to think you're on speed."

He shook his head and squinted. "You completely underestimate
my power with the ladies, little Leo."

"I don't know. I've seen you struggle with charm."

He scowled. "Bullshit."

I laughed at how easily it was to fool him into insecurity. "Okay. I
mean…Lana said… You know what? Never mind."

His scowl deepened, and now, I was the one laughing. "What did
she say?"

"Nothing."

Properly put back in line and officially sporting a scowl, he followed me contritely out of the locker room and down the hall to the
fan area, and it didn't take long to spot Gemma and Alma.

Alma had somehow found a chair, and everyone around her was
keeping clear. Apparently, she'd been showing off her personality.

Cam and I moved quickly, and I scooped Gemma into my arms
and settled my lips on hers. She broke it off quickly, glancing to Alma,
and I rolled my eyes.

Like my sex-toy-peddling aunt cared about us kissing.

Cam took the opportunity, however, to cut in.

"Hi, ladies. I'm Cam. Leo's one and only best friend."

I rolled my eyes as Gemma and Alma smiled.

"He's a pain in my ass," I said in response, and Alma smacked me.

"Be nice, Leonard."

Oh no. I do not like that light in Cam's eyes.

"Yeah, Leonard," Cam said then, and I sighed. *Great.* It looked like that name would never, ever die a proper death. Before long, the whole team would be calling me it. "Your girl and your aunt came all this way to see you play."

Back on topic, I turned to Gemma and smiled. "That's true. I can't believe you guys came."

"Well," Nonna cut in without remorse, "I actually had someone to help me get here. If you'd thought of it sooner, I might have made it to a few more games."

Cam smiled, absolutely swimming in all his glory as she knocked me down peg after peg. "Yeah, Leonard."

I sighed.

"I wish I'd known you guys were coming. I have to take the bus back, and I can't stay to hang out."

Gemma smiled, and as pretty as it was, it wasn't the easy one I'd come to know. "That's okay. Alma and I have *plans*."

"That's right," Nonna interjected before I had to ask. "We're going to check out a few stores."

"*Stores?*" I mouthed to Gemma.

She nodded solemnly, and I shivered.

I really didn't want to think about my great-aunt visiting sex shops with my girlfriend, but I doubted Gemma was any more thrilled to be going to them. Out of the two, I definitely had the lesser of the evils.

"I guess I'll see you when we get back home, then?" I asked hopefully, and Gemma nodded. I desperately wanted more quality time with her. More kissing, more sex, more *Gemma*.

We were just getting to the point where I could ask her to sing for me at home without it being a sore spot. Up until now, we'd both pretty much avoided the topic completely.

After a quick round of goodbyes, I shook off Cam's hand as he put it on the small of the back to escort me to the bus.

He laughed, of course, happy to be able to tease me in private again.

"So, I guess you and the piss-pouring princess made up again?"

I rolled my eyes.

"Yes. A long time ago. I just pushed too hard."

"What do you mean?"

"With the gig. At Monarchy. She wasn't ready."

Cam pursed his lips thoughtfully as we walked toward the bus, and I got lost in my thoughts. It wasn't until we climbed on board and sat down that he spoke again. But when he did, he was serious.

"You know, sometimes people *need* the push. I don't know the details, but if you believe what you did was the right thing, I wouldn't back down."

My brain spun as I considered his words and weighed my options.

Could I go on as we were and just leave it alone?

Or did I believe in Gemma enough to give her the push?

And most importantly…could I really handle the consequences?

I'd take my time. But eventually, I would have to decide.

Gemma deserved the world.

And the world, well, it fucking deserved Gemma's voice.

Chapter Twenty-Nine

Gemma

I couldn't believe I was here, sitting inside Baltimore's stadium, watching the Mavericks fight for every inch against Philadelphia's offense.

I'd never been so invested in a sports game in my entire life.

But I guessed that's what happened when your boyfriend just so happened to be a professional football star.

One day, you barely knew the difference between a touchdown and a field goal, and the next, you were shouting profanities at the refs for shitty penalty calls against your team.

Leo's team.

I'd only made it to one of their four play-off games, but thanks to my intimate connections to one of the very players on that field, I was a spectator for the Mavericks' biggest game of the year. The entire professional football league's biggest game of the year, in fact.

Time was ticking off the clock, and all I could do was fidget and bounce around on my feet as I watched what would most likely be one of the final plays of the game.

The anticipation of it all nearly took my breath away.

Fourth quarter. Third down.

One lone minute left on the clock.

The Mavericks led by seven points, and Philadelphia had the ball.

The entire stadium grew to a quiet hush as the guys lined up on the fifteen-yard line, and my heart started to pound rapidly inside of my chest.

This was it. The championship game.

And all the Mavericks had to do was hold Philadelphia off for one minute.

Sixty fucking seconds and the trophy would be theirs after years of coming up short. Obviously, I hadn't been following it that long, but my relationship with Leo had changed things. He'd been explicit in the details he shared with me about the guys and what this meant to them.

I only really had the firsthand experience of witnessing how much it meant to him. But if it meant even a fifth to other guys of what it meant to Leo, I couldn't imagine what the entire team must be feeling.

Some of them, Cam included, had been after this title for their entire careers. Years of sweat and agony, years of putting it all on the line, years of coming so close they could taste it.

And now, they had a real fucking shot.

I spotted number twenty-one on the field, and my chest grew tight with nerves and adoration.

C'mon, Leo!

Fuck, I was nervous for him. And when I looked over at the wives and girlfriends of Leo's teammates, I quickly realized I wasn't the only one who was freaking out.

Quinn Bailey's wife Cat was literally sitting on the edge of her seat.

Lana Simone, Cam's fiancée, stood by the glass of the box, her elbows resting on the railing and her eyes wide with anticipation.

And Six Phillips bounced around the VIP box with her camera in one hand and a tiny infant in the other arm, catching everything and everyone on film.

Philly's quarterback took the hike, and the players on the line barreled toward each other.

With a short, lateral pass to his left, Philadelphia's QB got rid of the ball and the receiver snagged it from the air, but he only managed a yard or two before the Mavericks defense tackled his ass to the ground.

Hell yes!

Everyone—including me—inside the VIP box was on their feet, screaming and cheering and clapping and high-fiving each other.

And we were practically docile compared to the crowd in the stands. They jived and jumped and rumbled so loud, goose bumps peppered the skin of my arms.

"C'mon, Mavericks!" Lana shouted through cupped hands. "You got this, guys!"

"Let's go, Mavs!" Six exclaimed.

The ref verified fourth down with a wave of his arms and a blow of his whistle, and the crowd went wild.

With thirty seconds left on the clock, Philly either needed to score a touchdown or gain eight yards for another first down. And my man was one of the key players assigned to stop them.

Both teams lined up.

When the quarterback grabbed the snap, I gripped the edges of my seat as I watched the play unfold.

Philly's QB looked left, he looked right, then he repeated that circuit again with the ball in his hands until, thanks to Leo and the rest of the team's coverage, he ran out of viable options. In a last-ditch effort, he cradled the ball to his chest and attempted the run himself.

One yard. Two yards. He pivoted and twisted and tried like hell to get past the Mavs offense, but when he reached the ten-yard line, Leo was there. Just like he trained me to know he'd been trained, he wrapped both arms around the QB's back and pulled him straight to the ground with a clashing bang.

"Yes! Yes! Yes!" I shouted at the top of my lungs as I hopped up from my seat.

As the big bruiser of a quarterback hit the ground, the ball popped out from his chest and bounced across the grass.

Collins, a defensive end for our team, snagged the ball from the ground and headed toward the Mavs end zone.

By the time he reached the thirty-yard line, Philly's offense managed to stop his progress with a quick tackle and pileup, but it was too late. The writing was on the wall, and the news was on the scoreboard.

The New York Mavericks, your national champions!

The stadium vibrated so hard, I thought the center would cave in, and confetti fell from the sky. And Leo and his teammates? They were losing their ever-loving shit.

My heart swelled with pride, and tears pricked my eyes. They deserved this. They'd worked so hard. *Leo* had worked so *hard*.

God, I couldn't fucking wait to get to him.

Only about an hour of being a dutiful girlfriend while he had his moment with the team and about a hundred reporters and I'd be able to.

I didn't mind. Watching him out there was like watching him come alive.

The guys had taken the stage and accepted their trophy, Leo's face making more than one appearance on the JumboTron, handsome smile and all, and the television sportscaster had done the presentation and interview. The celebration was still wild, but we'd finally reached my favorite part, and that was because we, friends and family, were finally allowed down on the field to celebrate with them. I'd finally get to wrap my arms around my favorite Mavericks player.

My Leo.

The instant my shoes hit the grass, I spotted him standing near a few of his teammates and went sprinting toward the group with the biggest grin on my face.

"Leo!" I shouted, and he turned around.

The instant our eyes locked, the biggest, most infectious smile took over his face.

He caught me in his arms and lifted me up off my feet, and I secretly hoped my feet never hit earth again.

"Congratulations, Leonard!" I giggled and wrapped my arms and legs around his body as he slowly spun us around in a circle. "You did so fucking awesome!"

Leo's baby-blue eyes met mine, and I didn't miss the way they lit up his face in the most perfect way. It was like being able to put a candle inside the ocean without having the flame go out.

"Fuck, I'm so happy you're here," he whispered into my ear right before he put his hand in my hair and pressed his mouth to mine.

"Me too," I told him honestly. "Watching you out there, Leo, it was something else. I've never seen anything like it in my life."

His smile changed then, slipping to the side a little with a wonkiness I couldn't place. I didn't know why, but it felt like something had just moved through him.

I was probably just imagining it. With a shake of his head, he picked me up and swung me around again and pressed his lips to mine.

There was only one thing that could make this day better, and I knew it was coming. Being alone.

Silently, I thanked my lucky stars that I'd made this road trip by myself.

Alma had decided to sit this game out and watch it from home. Apparently, she was "too old and decrepit" to handle the wild celebrations that would ensue after the Mavericks won. But, she'd sent me an excited text filled with only emojis the instant they were titled this year's champions.

And Leo's parents hadn't made it to the game either, a fact that I had a hard time wrapping my head around. But apparently, they were on an anniversary cruise they'd had planned for a year. Ye of little faith, I guess they'd had doubts the Mavericks would end up in the Championship in his rookie season. But even without them, we weren't exactly lacking for company.

The entire team, their families, the owner and his family and friends, along with the entire staff of Mavericks Stadium were a raging group of lunatics around us, and I had a feeling the group party wouldn't be ending anytime soon.

Maybe that was why celebrating tonight at the hotel was just about all I could think about. And with the mischief in Leo's eyes lighting up the ten feet around us, I had a feeling I wasn't the only one.

When the hotel door finally clicked shut behind us five hours later, I sighed in relief.

It wasn't so much that I hadn't enjoyed the boisterous celebration of a Mavericks championship team that had been years and years in the making, it was simply that I was ready for one-on-one time with my man.

He was happy. I was happy.

And I imagined the celebration sex tonight was going to be out of this fucking world.

With a twist and a heavy breath, he fell back on the bed and splayed out like a sea star as I slid the lock and chain home on the door.

I laughed at him softly and closed the distance, climbing up onto the bed between his legs and leaning down to press our chests together.

He grabbed on to my hips and smiled the smile of a man who had everything.

"Happy, baby?" I asked, wanting to hear him say it, even though

I most definitely knew the answer.

"You have no idea." He shook his head almost manically and burst out in laughter. "I just can't believe it really happened. National champions, Gem! Can you fucking believe it?"

I smiled and kissed his lips before settling my weight back into my knees and answering gleefully. "Of course, I can. You're magic out there, Leo."

His smile went wonky for the second time that day, and now that we were in the privacy of our hotel room, I figured there wouldn't be any harm in finding out why.

I wanted to know what he was thinking, *everything* he was thinking.

"What's that look?" I asked, smoothing my thumb over the wrinkle in his brow as I did.

He adjusted his face. "What look?"

Ah, okay. So, he was going to deny it. I could play games if he wanted to.

"Don't play innocent with me, silly boy," I teased. "This is the second time I've seen it today. There was a look, you know there was a look, and I can be relentless when I want to be. So, why don't you do us both a favor and just tell me?"

I laughed at my pushiness and expected him to do the same, so when he sat up underneath me and cleared his throat, it came as a bit of a surprise.

I shifted to the side to keep from falling off onto the floor, and he ran a hand through his hair.

"Leo," I said, much more seriously now. "What's going on?"

He nodded to himself and turned to face me before reaching out to grab my hands, and a fucking clawing feeling took up residence in my throat.

Good God, what was going on?

"You're scaring me."

"Okay, okay," he said then, finally pulling my hands to his chest and opening his lungs. "Okay, so hear me out. Today, you got to watch me do something I love, right?"

"Right."

"And it was special for you, wasn't it?"

I nodded, completely baffled. "Of course."

"Well…Gem. God, I can't believe I'm doing this tonight of all nights."

"Leo," I said, my stomach officially in my throat.

"But that's what it's like for me watching you perform music."

Oh no. No, no, no, no. Not this. Not right now.

"Leo—"

"It *is*," he insisted. "I know you're scared, but I was scared once too. I didn't think I'd be able to do this, and look at me now. We won the fucking Championship! You can do it! I know you can!"

"Leo!"

"That's why I booked you another shot at Monarchy. I know you weren't ready before, but I've given you time—"

Emotions on overload, I jumped up from the bed on a scream and ripped my hands from his.

"I cannot believe you did this again!" I yelled, shaking so hard I could barely breathe. "Didn't you learn anything last time?"

"Yes!" he yelled back, his temper fully engaged now too. "I learned that you're way too stubborn for your own good! God, Gemma, why can't you let me help you? Why can't you give yourself a shot?"

My bones ached and my heart pounded and everything in me screamed at myself to give it more time. Not to make another mess out of this. To be calm and rational.

But I was drained dry, and I didn't have any waiting left to give.

This time, he'd pushed too far.

The walls closed in around me, and anxiety wrapped her fingers around my throat like a fucking vise.

"I may be stubborn, but I'm allowed to be. This is my life!"

"Oh yeah? I thought maybe we were building something where it might be *our* life!"

"Not anymore," I said, my voice as soft as a church mouse but as effective as a bullet.

My words had been a gut-punch reaction, flying out of my mouth and past my lips before I could really process them.

But I'd said it, and I couldn't take it back. And by the devastated look on his face, I knew I could never fix whatever I'd destroyed with those two measly but fucking powerful words.

He took a step back, and before I knew it, I found myself taking fifteen steps away from him.

Leo didn't say anything. And I didn't know what to say.

Honestly, I didn't have anything left to offer or any piece of my heart left to break.

He'd pushed me past the point of no return, and all I could do was finish the distance toward the door.

Out of the room.

Out of Leo's life.

As the door clicked shut behind me, a sob bubbled up from my throat.

I covered my mouth with my hand, and I walked toward the elevator, trying like hell not to make eye contact with any passersby in the hall.

Once I reached the lobby, I made my way outside to hail a cab.

That night, I might've physically left the hotel, but my heart stayed behind, battered and bloodied and broken and, still, with Leo.

But it didn't matter. None of it mattered. A permanent line in the sand had been drawn.

And that line, well, it severed the ties between Leo and me for good.

Chapter Thirty

Leo

Cameras flashed and people cheered as the Championship victory parade through midtown Manhattan carried on around us. I'd never seen this kind of fanfare, and I'd never enjoyed it *less*.

Goddamn, I'd never known I could do something as momentous as win the Championship during my rookie season as a pro footballer and still be so unhappy. The whole city was out here to celebrate—the fucking mayor had dedicated the day to us—and it all still seemed incomplete.

How fucking pathetic.

"Dude, cheer the fuck up," Sean said, shoving me in the back as the float moved on between 34th and 35th streets. "You're ruining the group picture."

Cam nodded as I looked back at him, and it took all I had not to hit him in the fucking face. *Some people need the push, Leo*, he'd said.

Fucking bastard.

But given the huge crowd of people and this being a professional outing and all with little kids lining the streets, I lashed out verbally instead of hitting him. "This is all your fucking fault anyway."

"My fault?" Cam said on a jerk of his whole body. "How the hell is your PMS my fault?"

"Because you're the one who said I should push Gemma. That people *needed* to be pushed. You're the reason we're not together."

His face softened a little at my raw emotion, but his resolve didn't. Not even a little. "Sorry, dude, but you're going to have to turn that finger around. I may have given the advice, but the advice was sound. If you know in your heart that she needed a push, this is a part of the process."

"What the fuck do you mean? A part of the process?"

Cam and Sean smiled and waved, but I'd given up all pretense as I turned around to face them. In my mind, I knew it was ridiculous to be having this conversation here, in the middle of our Championship victory parade, but I couldn't help it. I had to feel some sort of closure. I had to get some sort of answers.

And these fuckers seemed to think they had some. So they were gonna speak up whether they wanted to or not.

"Well?" I prompted, when neither of them spoke quickly enough.

Cam almost smiled, and the urge to hit him no matter where we were got a little stronger. "I mean that just because you're broken up now doesn't mean you're broken up forever. I think the real tough stuff, the stuff that *has* to happen, sometimes needs a rocky road to build the foundation."

I squinted my eyes and my head spun. Before I knew it, I was turning to Sean with a scowl on my face.

He laughed.

"He's saying that after breakups can come makeups. Your girl is scared, dude. But are you sure she needs to do the thing you're pushing her to do?"

I thought about it. Hard.

Pushed past the heartache and the pain and really laid out the facts in my mind.

Gemma had the voice, the look, and the star quality. But beyond that, she had the passion. I never, ever saw her light up the way she did when she was onstage anywhere else.

God, even when we'd shared quiet moments at home together, I'd never seen her look more at peace, more herself, than when she was fiddling around with her guitar and writing lyrics in one of her numerous notebooks.

Music was her fucking life, whether she wanted to admit it or not.

My answer was confident as I recited it back to them. "She was born to do it."

Both of them shrugged, shared a look, and then turned back to me. "Then you know what you have to do," Cam said.

"No," I said with a laugh. "No, I don't."

"When did you set up the performance for?"

"Tomorrow night."

"Did you cancel it?"

"No."

"Don't," Cam said, clear and certain.

"What do you mean, don't? What exactly am I supposed to do if she doesn't show up?"

"I guess you better work on your performance skills, then," Sean said with a laugh.

Ha-ha, very funny. "I'm serious."

"So am I," Cam said frankly. "Give her the chance. Give her the opportunity to come through when someone believes in her even more than she believes in herself."

Give her the chance.

Turning around to take my position on the float and wave to the crowd, I thought about their words and ran them through my mind like a carefully sorted conveyor in a factory.

I had the tools to give Gemma the confidence she needed. But until she got there, I just needed to be the one to have the confidence for her.

Sure, it might be a shitshow if she didn't show up, but I knew, by the time the parade ended, I *knew* I had to give it a shot.

Pulling out my phone and dialing a number I couldn't even believe I had, I waited as it rang.

Abby, an apparent phone ninja as well as apartment squatter, answered nearly immediately.

"It's about time you called me," she greeted, and just like that, I felt affirmed that I was doing the right thing. She'd put my number in her phone for a reason, and she'd known Gemma even longer than I had. If the two of us thought this was right, it had to be.

"I'm not canceling the performance tomorrow night," I told her simply. "Tell Gemma that I'll be waiting for her, and that I can't wait to hear her sing."

"Anything else?" she said, a smile in her voice.

"Tell her...just...make it clear I believe in her. And well...make it clear I love her."

My eyes bugged out as I realized what I'd just said, but it was entirely too late to take it back. It wasn't the most romantic way to out your love for someone, but it sure as shit was the truth.

"Don't worry, Romeo," Abby said with a laugh. "I'll tell her. And for the record?"

"Yeah?"

"Both of those things are more than clear to me. But if I have anything to do with it, you're going to have the chance to tell her yourself."

Chapter Thirty-One

Gemma

I'd felt off all day. Nauseated, panicky, and incredibly anxious.

And I'd done everything I could to distract myself.

I went for a run across the Brooklyn Bridge.

And, it should be noted, if you haven't "gone for a run" in two years, the Brooklyn Bridge is the very last place to start. By the time I'd gotten back to my apartment, I was panting like a dog, the muscles in my legs had congealed, and I was calling myself every name under the sun.

But even after that, sea legs and all, I'd kept myself moving.

I ran errands.

I did laundry.

I cleaned my apartment.

I even paid my fucking bills two weeks before they were due.

Basically, I'd worked through to-do lists for the next three years.

But, to my utter disappointment, nothing made me feel better.

And, even though I didn't want to admit it to myself, I knew why.

Well, thanks to Abby and her meddling, I knew it because she hadn't stopped talking about it for the past twenty-four hours.

How she'd found out? I didn't have a fucking clue, nor did I want to engage in the conversation that would give me the answers.

But I knew. *I fucking knew.*

Tonight was *the* night. The gig at Monarchy.

As the hours passed and the eight o'clock call time that Leo had put on the books for me neared, I couldn't stop thinking about it.

I couldn't stop thinking about *him.*

And the more I thought about him, the more I doubted walking away from him.

The more I questioned my reaction to his meddling.

The more I wondered if I'd done the right thing.

And, ultimately, the more confused and emotional I became.

At a little after five, I sat down on my couch with a bowl of instant mac and cheese to watch reruns of *Friends,* and I'd never felt so fucking pathetic in my life.

Not to mention, instant mac and cheese *always* tastes like burned cheese with a hint of plastic, and I was in such a sad sack mind-set that even Ross shouting "Pivot! Pivot!" didn't make me laugh.

Fuck, I felt low.

Probably the lowest I'd ever felt in my life.

But I didn't know what to do or how to change it.

A part of me wanted to call Leo.

And even a teeny tiny part of me wanted to just show up at the gig.

But the anxiety-ridden, scared as fuck part of me refused to loosen the reins.

Once Ross brought his couch back to the furniture store in two pieces, I tossed my half-eaten bowl of cheesy plastic and grabbed the remote to find something else to watch.

Who knows how long I sat there mindlessly flipping through the channels, but when three knocks resonated from my front door, I blinked out of my daze and glanced over my shoulder and toward the entryway.

Surely, I was hearing things, right?

I mean, I wasn't expecting any visitors.

And the only visitor I could expect never knocked.

Three more knocks and I slowly got up from the couch and walked to the entryway. When I looked into the peephole and saw Abby standing on the other side, I opened the door and furrowed my brow. "Uh… What is happening right now?"

"What do you mean?"

"You're knocking," I said, and she stared at me in confusion.

"And that's a problem because…?"

"You never knock," I explained. "You mysteriously end up in my apartment, but you never knock."

"Are you going to let me in?" she asked, ignoring the rest of my plight. Without the energy to stand there and argue, I propped the door open.

She walked inside, and I followed her lead into the living room.

"Jesus Christ, it smells terrible in here," she said and I shrugged.

"I made mac and cheese."

"Instant?"

"Yeah."

"That explains it," Abby said with a knowing smile.

But to my surprise, she didn't plop her ass down on my couch.

Instead, she walked into the hallway and straight into my bedroom.

"Uh… What are you doing?" I called toward her.

"Making sure you're ready to go!"

"Ready to go where?"

She peeked her head out of my bedroom. "You fucking know where."

"I'm not going to the gig," I said, but Abby just ignored me and went back to whatever she was doing.

Eventually, I became too curious not to walk into my bedroom.

She stood beside my bed, and I watched in annoyance as she packed up my guitar in its case.

"Stop doing that," I said, but she ignored me.

"You need to get dressed."

"I'm not going anywhere, Abby."

Once she had my guitar packed up, she moved her focus toward my closet and started pulling out clothes and tossing them onto my bed. "Dress? Skirt? Jeans? What are you feeling for tonight, sweet cheeks?"

"Abby," I said through a tight jaw and started to reverse her efforts by putting stuff back into my closet. "I'm not going to the gig."

Without the slightest bit of hesitation, she tossed whatever clothes were in her hands on top of my crumpled comforter and then gently shoved me onto my bed until my ass was firmly on the mattress.

"What are you doing?" I shrieked, but she stared down at me, completely unfazed.

"A goddamn intervention."

I opened my mouth to tell her to shove her intervention up her ass, and she held up a defiant hand. "You're going to stay quiet for two fucking minutes and listen to what I have to say, and if by the end of it, you still want to be an avoiding biotch, then I'll leave you to it, okay?"

I rolled my eyes. "Fine."

"I know the whole music thing is new for you," she started. "I know it's scary. I know your family is a fucking cockblock and a half, telling you shit like *music isn't a career*, but trust me when I say this, you have nothing to be insecure about, Gem. You are incredible. You're one in a million. Music *is* a career for you. And you sure as shit shouldn't be throwing away an opportunity like this just because you're feeling scared."

With clammy hands and a stream of sweat on my back, my body turned into a frozen log of panic as she laid it out. Giving in to this would mean confronting my family, and confronting my family would mean hours and hours and years of hard work until I made it happen. I refused to fail in the wake of their disappointment, only to come out of the deal with nothing. If I did this…if I started now…if I took this step…there was no turning back.

Screw the temp stuff and the steady paycheck, I'd have to dream-chase until I caught the fucker, no matter the consequences.

"This is important, Gem. It could be a huge turning point for you. And it is literally killing me to sit back and watch you throw it away."

My body shook as I fully considered what I was going to do. Was I really going to give myself a shot at my dream? *The real one.*

"Gem, if you don't go to that club tonight, if you don't get on that stage and sing a song and play your music and let everyone in that room see and hear how much talent you have, you are going to regret it," she said, and my chest tightened. "He called me, you know," she added, and her voice turned soft. "He called me in the hope that I could help make you realize you're making a big mistake. He called me because he cares about you and he wants to see you happy. He wants to see you live out your dreams, even though you refuse to admit them to yourself. And, most importantly, he called me because he loves you, Gem."

He loves me?

She nodded even though the words never left my lips. "He really, truly loves you, Gem. And God, please don't miss out on this opportunity. Please don't let this slip through your fingertips."

Tears pricked my eyes, and instantly, I knew she was right.

If I didn't go to Monarchy, I would regret it.

Because of the music.

And because of Leo.

And because dreams weren't built on fear. They were built on the courage you used to get over it.

I wanted my dream. I wanted music, and I wanted Leo.

From here on out, there was no turning back.

Chapter Thirty-Two

Leo

Three bands had already been on, and with each passing set, my sickness seemed to grow more and more in tune with the beat. On the plus side, if I upchucked right in the middle of it all, at least I would be on tempo.

Ah, fuck.

She wasn't here yet, I had no idea if she was coming, and if this didn't work out, I didn't know how to move on. Clearly, the pressure of it all was starting to get to me.

I'd been serious when I told Abby that I loved Gemma, but I wasn't exactly sure having her friend tell her for me was the best route of profession. Luckily, Abby'd made it seem like I'd get another chance.

Still, my pulse pounded and patrons laughed, and it was painfully obvious that as much as I felt like I couldn't breathe, the world was going on just fine around me.

Will Chambers was a nice guy, but he'd been breathing down my neck for the last twenty minutes while I'd stood backstage and offered up every prayer I could think of that Gemma would show. It was completely on him to fill this spot, and he didn't need some shit-stain kid like me ruining it for him.

And that was *not* me paraphrasing.

To make matters worse, Cam was busy tonight, so I was on my own, left to my fate like a lone reed blowing in the wind.

The only good news was that if she neglected to show, I could wallow in privacy.

"She's got five minutes, Leo," Will muttered in passing, and all I could do was nod.

I mean, I didn't know any better than he did if she was coming, and there wasn't a damn thing I could do about it.

But I'd resolved to believe in her, and I would keep doing it until all the time ticked away.

I watched the clock like punishment as the band onstage transitioned into their last song of the set and sweat pooled at my back.

One minute and thirty seconds left until my fate would be clear, and hell if it wasn't the fastest ninety seconds of my entire life.

One beat whirled into the next, and as the song came to a crashing crescendo, so did the love of my life.

The backstage door smashed open and she gulped at the air, but there, right in front of me, at the club, was the one and only Gemma Holden.

She'd shown up.

She'd shown up!

I'd shown up for her, and she'd shown up for me.

My heart made a bid to beat right out of my chest as she approached, wild-eyed and winded, and everything settled as she came to a stop.

"I'm scared out of my mind," she said without greeting or ado, and I didn't hesitate a moment longer. Quite frankly, there wasn't any time.

Wrapping my arms around her tightly, I pulled her to my chest and whispered the words I knew to be true directly into her ear.

"You're going to be great. I didn't have your music to give to the band to learn, so you're singing a song I know you know because I've heard it before. You mesmerized me with it, and you'll mesmerize them. You were born to do this, and I was born to be here for this moment."

"Leo," she said on a shaky whisper, and I hugged her tighter, holding on for dear life. If it weren't for the actual performance, I didn't know if I'd ever have been able to pry myself free.

"I love you, Gemma."

She pulled back fiercely, tears pricking her eyes as the words settled in.

I swallowed and nodded, ready to hear her say it back, and then Will swept in and ruined everything.

"Great. She's here. You're on, sweetheart. This way."

Without a moment's hesitation, he pulled her from my arms and toward the stage, and all I could do as she looked back at me was laugh.

Laugh at the comedy, laugh at the fact that I'd found the person I wanted to spend the rest of my life with and fucked up beyond royally in telling her the three most important words in the world.

If I were being frank, I'd fucked it up twice.

The opening bars of "Black Velvet" purred through the speakers as she took her place at the microphone, and I swallowed the lump in my throat. She shot one last glance back at me, the lights came up, the crowd quieted, and when the words started, so did Gemma.

Soft and sweet and the perfect pitch, her voice was everything I'd never heard from anyone on the music scene and then some, and the crowd was drawn into her trance with ease.

As the verses ticked on, she found her footing and a little more comfort, coming to life before all of our eyes.

Gone was the woman with the insecurities, and back was the one I'd seen in Drag and at the karaoke bar.

Back was the woman I'd fallen in love with.

Back was the woman Gemma was born to be.

I swayed and danced as everything right in the world came out of her mouth, and I laughed at the fact that I'd have to admit to Cam that he'd been right.

She'd needed the push. And I'd needed to be the one to do the pushing.

She and I were meant to be, and I couldn't think of anyone I'd rather spend my years in the spotlight with.

And I had no doubt she'd be in the spotlight.

If you please fell from her lips with ease and edge, and every single patron fell at her feet. As the lights came up and the song came to a close, the entire place took to their feet and took no pity on my ears. The roar was wild and the night was young, and as Gemma leaned into the microphone, I knew my life was just beginning.

Clear and steady, she said the words for everyone to hear.

"I love you too, Leo."

Funny how in a packed club full of people, it still felt like I was the only one she wanted listening.

Epilogue

Gemma

Five years later…

After the class's valedictorian finished up her inspirational speech, RIT's president stepped onto the stage, and my belly fluttered with excitement.

It was officially time. The big moment my handsome husband had been striving to reach for the past five years.

I'd watched him slave over term papers and fit in exams around football games.

I'd watched him take a full-time course load in the off-season.

I'd witnessed him do homework when we were in Fiji on our honeymoon and when he'd spent three months on a tour bus with me and my band.

Basically, I'd seen Leo never stop working toward his graduate degree goal, and finally, we were able to celebrate all of his hard work.

I smiled like a loon, but then my lips turned down at the corners as pain gripped my rounded stomach. I discreetly breathed through the discomfort while I placed a comforting hand to my hard as a rock belly.

Thirty-nine weeks pregnant with Leo's and my first child, and contractions had become a frequent occurrence in my life. According to my last doctor's visit with my OB/GYN, I was one centimeter dilated and our baby could make his or her arrival any day now.

I silently offered up a prayer that today would not be that day.

Tomorrow, though, that would be perfect.

But today, well, it was a big fucking day for my husband, and I didn't want to ruin it with an impromptu visit to the maternity ward.

Alma flashed me a side-eye and glanced down at my belly, but I forced a neutral smile to my lips to ease her curiosities.

It was just a few contractions. No big deal.

The university president spoke proudly into the mic. He talked about Leo's graduate class. He congratulated them on their victories and their hard work, but I couldn't quite focus on his words because my uterus apparently wanted all of my attention.

Another contraction gripped me tightly, and I pursed my lips into a tiny O and slowly breathed through the building pain.

Then the man at the mic proceeded to go into a long-winded, inspirational ramble about changing the world and shit, and I had two more contractions before he'd even paused to take a fucking breath.

But I was breathing. It was all I could manage to get through the uncomfortable fuckers.

Alma looked at me again, her lips pursed and her eyes narrowed as she homed in on my belly. She reached out and placed her hand against my stomach, and instantly, she looked up at me with a glare.

"How long have you been having these?" she asked, and I waved her off.

"It's not that bad."

"How long, Gemma?"

Even in her old age, the old biddy was still sharp as a tack.

"I don't know." I shrugged. "A few hours or so."

"A few hours?" she shouted, and everyone sitting around us, Leo's closest family and friends, turned their gazes toward us.

"Shut up, Nonna," I whisper-yelled. "I'm fine. It's fine. I promise."

She shook her head and pursed her lips again, but I averted my attention from her nosy ass and back toward the stage.

The graduate marshal had now taken the mic and had started to announce the graduates one by one as they took to the stage and accepted their diplomas.

He rolled through the alphabet only slightly quicker than my contractions rolled through my uterus, and by the time he reached the L's, I was thanking everything under the sun.

Graduation ceremonies inside a hot as balls auditorium while thirty-nine weeks pregnant was hard enough, but add in contractions that had turned painful, frequent, and consistent, and it felt like the longest minutes of my life.

Focus, Gem, I mentally coached myself.

And please, sweetheart, wait just a little bit longer, I silently whispered to the baby.

My husband had worked so hard for this moment, and I didn't want to do anything but celebrate this huge accomplishment with him.

I could focus on the contractions later.

But right now, I wanted to watch Leo get his diploma, and I didn't want anything to get in the way of that moment.

I spotted him in the sea of caps and gowns, and when he stood from his seat and lined up beside the stage, my heart fluttered inside my chest.

It's time, I thought to myself and smiled.

But that smile was quickly wiped away with a contraction, and it took everything in me not to grip an unknowing Cam Mitchell's shoulder and groan.

Thankfully, I kept my cool, and a good thirty seconds later, the contraction faded away and I had a moment of reprieve.

"Leonard Landry," the graduate marshal announced into the mic, and our little cheering section jumped to its feet.

"Leonard! Leonard! Leonard!" Cam, Sean, Quinn, and Teeny chanted together, their booming voices carrying over the noise of the crowd.

People in the auditorium turned in their seats to find the raucous commotion, but these guys gave zero fucks.

They cheered and clapped, and my heart swelled inside my chest as I watched my husband walk onto the stage.

Leo glanced up to his cheering section with a huge smile and waved toward us, and proud tears pricked my eyes.

"Hell yeah, Leonard!" Cam exclaimed once it had been made official with a shake of the dean's hand, a clench of his diploma between his fingertips, and a slide of his tassel from the right side of his cap to the left.

Alma took a goddamn air horn out of her neon-pink purse and startled the entire crowd.

Quinn put his fingers to his mouth and wolf-whistled, while his wife Cat adjusted their one-year-old daughter Callie on her hip and offered up her congratulations through a big smile and a clap of her hand against her thigh.

With a smile on Sean's lips and a GoPro in Six's hands, the two of them hooted their excitement toward the stage while Teeny helped their adorable son Fallon onto his shoulders so the little guy could get a better camera view of the ceremony.

Only five years old and already he was following in his momma's footsteps.

And me, well, I clapped like a lunatic.

Until another contraction gripped me so fucking hard that I had to clutch Cam's shoulder just to breathe through it.

"What the hell?" he muttered, but when he took in the strained lines of my face, his eyes turned wide. "Gem?" he questioned, and he glanced down at the free hand currently resting against the tight muscles of my belly. "Are you okay?"

"Uh-huh," I whispered through a panting breath, trying to play it off, but Alma didn't miss a fucking beat.

"Nope," she said. "She's not okay. She's in labor."

Our entire cheering section turned the gazes away from the stage, away from Leo's shining moment, and fixated their focus directly onto me and my overactive uterus.

"I'm fine," I said and held up what was supposed to be a reassuring hand. "I'm not in labor," I added. "It's just a few Braxton Hicks."

"Bullshit," Alma refuted and pulled her air horn back out of her purse and sounded the damn thing off a good five times. "Leonard!" she shouted at the top of her lungs.

Oh, for fuck's sake.

"Stop it, Nonna," I whispered through another building contraction. "Don't make a goddamn scene."

She ignored me completely, sounding off that fucking air horn again, and Leo looked up from where he'd just sat back down beside his classmates, and his eyes narrowed in confusion.

It was indisputable; his cheering section had officially gone wild.

Sure, none of us were topless or taking body shots off one another, but with the way his great-aunt kept firing off the air horn and scaring every goddamn person in the crowd, it probably wouldn't take long before security made an appearance beside our row.

"Leonard! Get your shit, and let's go!" she shouted again, but this time, she wasn't the only one yelling toward my extremely confused husband.

Sean and Cam had joined in.

"We need to get Gemma to the hospital!

"The baby is coming!"

I watched as understanding covered my husband's face, and it didn't take long before he was hopping up from his seat and running across the auditorium floor like a bat out of hell.

Of course, by that point, people in the audience had grown hip to our embarrassing game. Hell, some even pulled out phones and started recording the shenanigans that included several top players for the Mavericks helping a panting, pregnant lady out of her seat and toward the exit route.

We'd officially fucked up the whole damn graduation, and I was certain I'd find my beet-red and panting face splashed across *TMZ* or some shit.

But the contractions kept coming faster and stronger, and I didn't have much time to contemplate the media reaction we'd receive from this.

Our little cheering section had turned into a "Get Gemma to the hospital section," and by the time we reached the exit doors, Leo had met us there on a sprint.

The concern on his face had my heart clenching in discomfort.

"Baby, are you okay?" he asked and placed both of his hands onto my belly.

"I promise I tried to wait," I whispered, and tears started to spill from my eyes. "I tried to make the baby hold out a little longer so I didn't ruin your big day. I'm so sorry," I said just as my tears turned to full-on sobs.

"*Baby.*" Leo smiled down at me as he pulled me into his arms. "I can promise you that a graduation ceremony doesn't even come close to comparing to the day I get to meet our baby," he whispered into my ear.

I sniffled and nodded and buried my face in his shoulder.

When another contraction gripped my belly, I had to step back from my husband's comforting embrace and place both hands on my stomach as I found my focus to breathe through it.

"Gem," Leo said softly as he put a strong arm around my shoulders. "What do you say we get you to the hospital?"

"Can I get an epidural?" I asked and he grinned.

"Yes."

"And can you make sure someone takes away Alma's air horn?"

He chuckled. "Trust me, it's already been made a priority."

Leo

For the first time since we'd arrived at the hospital, we were alone.

My parents had driven Alma home. And our friends, Gemma's parents, and Grandpa Joe had left about thirty minutes ago.

"I can't stop looking at him, Gem," I whispered as I stared down at the baby inside my wife's arms. He was hands down the most beautiful little human I'd ever laid eyes on.

A healthy baby boy that my beautiful, strong wife and I had created.

At eight pounds, six ounces and twenty-one inches long, Noah James Landry made his surprising debut into this world on the day that I officially graduated from grad school.

Gemma's labor had lasted all of two hours once we'd arrived at the hospital, which, from what her nurses had said, was like a fucking record for a first-time mom.

Apparently, my kid was already fast and agile and quite the go-getter.

"Me either." Gemma grinned up at me, and I watched as Noah wrapped his entire little fist around her pinkie finger. "I love him so much, Leo. More than I ever knew was possible."

"Me too, baby." I kissed her forehead and then pressed a soft kiss to Noah's. "Me too."

"I was kind of hoping you would've waited until tomorrow to make your big debut," she whispered toward him, and he cooed as he stretched out his little legs. "But God, I'm so happy you're here."

I couldn't have said it better myself.

With my whole world sitting right before my eyes, I couldn't imagine life getting any better than this.

I'd married the woman of my fucking dreams and created the most perfect little human being I'd ever seen.

I'd finally finished that fucking master's degree.

My career on the Mavericks' squad was still solid as a rock.

And my wife's music career was only just starting to take off.

After a six-month tour across the United States and two hit songs on the radio, Gemma Landry was becoming a household name in the music industry.

Thankfully, her success had made it pretty damn easy for her parents and Grandpa Joe to understand why Gemma's career path didn't end the way they'd originally thought. The night all three of them had been sitting beside me in the front row while her band played the Staples Center had been one hell of a validating and emotional moment for her. One I'd been more than proud to be a part of.

When Noah started to cry, I didn't hesitate to pull him into my arms and rock him back and forth a bit.

But the cries only came harder, and I looked at Gemma in confusion. "Is he hungry?" I asked and she shrugged.

"Honestly, I think he just needs his diaper changed," she said. "Check that first, and if he's still upset, I'll try to breastfeed him again."

I grinned down at my son as I moved him over to the plastic hospital bassinette and laid his tiny body down on the miniature mattress.

He kicked out his legs the instant I unswaddled his blanket, and when I removed his onesie and diaper, it was pretty apparent the little dude had in fact needed a bit of freshening up.

Only ten hours old and I was learning pretty quick that babies spent most of their time eating, shitting, and pissing.

I grabbed baby wipes and a fresh diaper from the drawer below his bassinette, but just before I could get my little guy all cleaned up, an arc of urine left his small body and hit me directly in the face.

"Ah, shit," I muttered, and with the help of baby wipes, I prevented the stream from hitting me directly in the eyes.

"What's wrong?" Gemma asked from the bed.

"Noah just pissed all over me."

The room turned silent until it wasn't.

My wife was laughing her ass off, and my son, well, he was crying again.

"Stop laughing," I muttered as I quickly cleaned up Noah again and put on a fresh diaper. "It's not that funny."

"Trust me, it is flipping hilarious." She giggled, and I glanced at her over my shoulder.

When I quirked a brow, she added, "You getting peed on by our baby? Yeah, I'm having some serious déjà vu moments over here. Not to mention, I think it's safe to say Noah is one hundred percent *our* son."

And then the memory hit me.

That fateful day I'd met the woman of my dreams.

While it'd been slightly tainted, it had been the best fucking day of my life.

It had changed *everything.*

She had changed everything.

Yeah. I was certain life couldn't get any better than this.

THE END

Surely, you're ready for MORE Max Monroe books, right?
Don't worry, friends. Just because our favorite Mavericks Series has
come to an end, don't think we're not prepared to bring you more
hilarious, sexy, and fun rom-com.

2018 has been the start of ALL THE FUN THINGS.
And with 2019 just around the corner, we're only just getting started!
Find out why everyone is laughing their ass off every Monday
morning with us.
Max Monroe's Monday Morning Distraction.
It's hilarity and entertainment in newsletter form.
Trust us, you don't want to miss it.
Stay up-to-date with our characters, us, and get your own copy of
Monday Morning Distraction by signing up for our newsletter:
http://www.authormaxmonroe.com/#!contact/c1kcz
You may live to regret much, but we promise it won't be this.
If you're already signed up, consider sending us a message to tell us
how much you love us. We really like that. ;)

Follow us online:

Website: www.authormaxmonroe.com

Facebook: www.facebook.com/authormaxmonroe

Reader Group: www.facebook.com/groups/1561640154166388

Twitter: www.twitter.com/authormaxmonroe

Instagram: www.instagram.com/authormaxmonroe

Goodreads: goo.gl/8VUIz2

Bookbub: www.bookbub.com/authors/max-monroe

Acknowledgments

First of all, THANK YOU for reading. That goes for anyone who's bought a copy, read an ARC, helped us beta, edited, or found time in their busy schedule to help us out in any way.

Thank you for supporting us, for talking about our books, and for just being so unbelievably loving and supportive of our characters. You've made this our MOST favorite adventure thus far.

THANK YOU to Basil and Banana.

THANK YOU to our amazing readers.

THANK YOU to all of you awesome and supportive bloggers.

THANK YOU to our editor, Lisa.

THANK YOU to our agent, Amy.

THANK YOU to Jenn and Sarah and Brooke and everyone else at Social Butterfly PR.

THANK YOU to our Camp Love Yourself Members.

THANK YOU to Kristina and our Thatchlings.

And last, but certainly not least, THANK YOU to our family.

Max: Another short and sweet acknowledgment?

Monroe: Yep. You bet ya. We've got a baby to deliver and our next big project to—

Max: *We've* got a baby to deliver?

Monroe: Metaphorically, yes.

Max: And what about physically?

Monroe: Well, all I can say is good luck, friend.

Max: [laughs] Wow. Thanks for the vote of confidence.

Monroe: [grins] You're going to be great. Your epidural is going to make you feel zero pain, and your baby is going to be beautiful.

Max: [nods] I like where this is headed. Keep going…

Monroe: Like, legit, right after the delivery, you'll be sitting there in your hospital bed looking like Kim Kardashian's Glam Squad just did your hair and makeup. And your baby is just going to be smiling up at you. It's going to be some Hallmark Moment kind of shit.

Max: [rubs belly] That's way better.

Monroe: [laughs] I figured you'd like that.

Max: So, now what do we do?

Monroe: Well…we finish up writing that one book with that one guy who is…*you know…*

Max: Oh yes…*I know…* [grins]

Monroe: And then we go on maternity leave.

Max: You mean, I go on maternity leave.

Monroe: Yeah, that's what I said.

Max: You said we.

Monroe: Nooooo… [smiles] Pretty sure I said you. Anyway, enough chitchat, we've got other priorities to focus on.

Max: Like what?

Monroe: Lunch.

Max: Now that is something my baby and I can get behind!

Thank you to everyone we love and adore!

Our readers, our bloggers, our fellow authors, our entire team, just everyone!

We love you tons and tons and tons!

Thank you for letting us do what we love every single day.

XOXO,
Max Monroe

Made in the USA
Coppell, TX
07 March 2020

16608663R00128